A DANGEROUS REFUGE

Emma Ashcroft comes to Rotterdam with a decision to make. Is she in love with fun-loving Danny Lockwood, or is their relationship over? Danny is not at the station to meet her, and then, from his high-rise apartment, Emma witnesses his abduction by two mysterious strangers. Could Steven Reeves, who claims to represent the landlord, help her — and can she trust him? Will Emma survive danger, deceit and betrayal to discover the truth — and true love?

Books by Anne Hewland in the Linford Romance Library:

STOLEN SECRET
TO TRUST A STRANGER
A SUBTLE DECEIT
BLIGHTED INHERITENCE

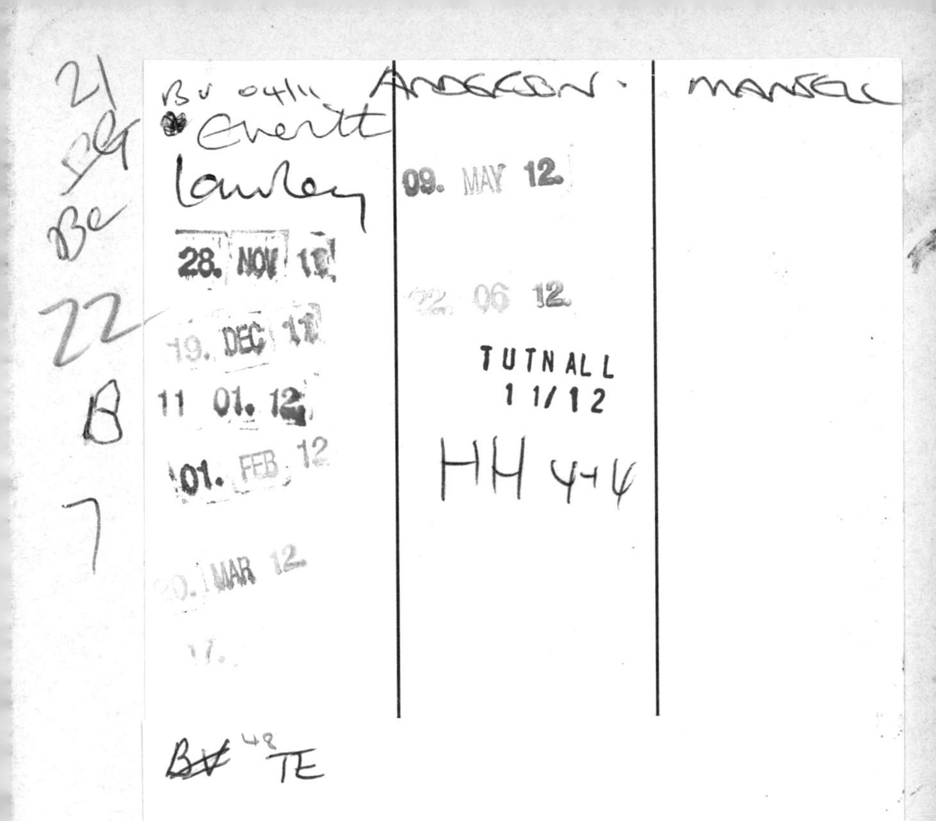

worcestershire
countycouncil
Libraries & Learning

700033242708

SPECIAL MESSAGE TO READERS

This book is published under the auspices of

THE ULVERSCROFT FOUNDATION

(registered charity No. 264873 UK)

Established in 1972 to provide funds for research, diagnosis and treatment of eye diseases. Examples of contributions made are: —

A Children's Assessment Unit at Moorfield's Hospital, London.

•

Twin operating theatres at the Western Ophthalmic Hospital, London.

•

A Chair of Ophthalmology at the Royal Australian College of Ophthalmologists.

•

The Ulverscroft Children's Eye Unit at the Great Ormond Street Hospital For Sick Children, London.

You can help further the work of the Foundation by making a donation or leaving a legacy. Every contribution, no matter how small, is received with gratitude. Please write for details to:

THE ULVERSCROFT FOUNDATION,
The Green, Bradgate Road, Anstey,
Leicester LE7 7FU, England.
Telephone: (0116) 236 4325

In Australia write to:
THE ULVERSCROFT FOUNDATION,
c/o The Royal Australian and New Zealand
College of Ophthalmologists,
94-98 Chalmers Street, Surry Hills,
N.S.W. 2010, Australia

ANNE HEWLAND

A DANGEROUS REFUGE

Complete and Unabridged

LINFORD
Leicester

First published in Great Britain in 2009

First Linford Edition
published 2010

British Library CIP Data

Hewland, Anne.
A dangerous refuge.- -
(Linford romance library)
1. Kidnapping- -Netherlands- -Rotterdam- -
Fiction. 2. Romantic suspense novels.
3. Large type books.
I. Title II. Series
823.9′2–dc22

ISBN 978–1–44480–375–4

Published by
F. A. Thorpe (Publishing)
Anstey, Leicestershire

Set by Words & Graphics Ltd.
Anstey, Leicestershire
Printed and bound in Great Britain by
T. J. International Ltd., Padstow, Cornwall

This book is printed on acid-free paper

1

Emma heaved her bag across the busy concourse of Rotterdam Central Station with mixed feelings of guilt and pleasure — and Danny wasn't there. No, of course he wasn't. Why had she thought he would do something so predictable as to make an arrangement and stick to it? She peered through the hurrying crowds, hoping that at any moment he would appear. It would be just like him to leap out unexpectedly. Danny was so much fun to be with, so full of surprising plans. You never knew what was going to happen next. And whatever he did it was always with a smile that made you feel weak at the knees.

She sighed, looking round anxiously. Yes, he was fun and she loved being with him. But was that enough? Sometimes she wasn't sure she knew

Danny, not deep down. She frowned. And how did she really feel about him? He had never seemed to be in England long enough for her to find out. She missed him when his work took him away to various destinations across Europe — although she had never been too clear about what his work actually entailed.

Lately she'd begun to feel that she couldn't define her feelings and that something was missing. Perhaps he had picked up on her restlessness because for once he had responded to her disappointment when he had a call, yet again, to fly off at a moment's notice.

'Okay, babe, come over to Rotterdam for a week,' he had said. 'I'll go first. Just give me a few days to sort one or two things. I'll meet you at the station.'

Yes. She hadn't had to think twice. But she knew that seeing Danny in one of his other base locations, as he put it, would be what she needed to make her decision. By the end of this week, she promised herself, she would have made her mind up. If she decided to ditch him, her mum and her happily-married older sisters would be only too pleased; she knew that. Though maybe she needed to get away from their influence, too. They didn't approve of Danny and never had. And she had to be honest with herself, perhaps that had been part of the attraction . . .

She took out her mobile phone.

'Em!' He sounded surprised. And not entirely pleased, she thought.

'Had you forgotten I was coming?' She made her voice teasing.

'No, of course not. I wasn't expecting you so early. That coach from the ferry never arrives at the time it's supposed to.'

'And today it has.'

'Yes. That's good. No hold up with customs or anything?'

'No. Isn't that more likely when you go home again?'

He didn't answer her question, was moving on to something else now.

'It's just that — well, I have to see

some people. Didn't want to, not today. Not when my best girl is arriving. You'll be the toast of the town.' The happy, teasing note was back in his voice now. She must have imagined the doubt. 'Tell you what, babe — can you hang on for an hour? Or better still, go and have a coffee or something? There's a good place on the main road, turn left and on the right. You'll be okay there. With your luggage.' He gave a name Emma didn't catch. 'When I've got rid of them, I'll phone you again. See you. Love you. 'Bye.'

'But — ' Emma stared at the phone. 'My bag's heavy,' she muttered. 'I don't want to be carting it about all morning.' And it would have been lighter if the bag hadn't also included a hefty package apparently full of Danny's essential paperwork that he had wanted her to include at the last minute. She hadn't felt too keen about that at the time. Okay, she told herself, she'd been going out with Danny long enough to know that resourcefulness was often called for. And she didn't particularly want to sit drinking coffee for an hour — even if she'd managed to catch the name of the café he'd mentioned. Something Dutch that had sounded like a grunt. No, she would find the left luggage lockers and explore the city herself.

Of course, she didn't have suitable coins for the locker and had to cash in one of her notes in the shop, trying to work out which purchase would give the most useful amount of change. The confectionery mostly had English-looking logos and names — almost familiar, but with subtle differences.

She couldn't hear anyone speaking English around her, but knew from Danny that the Dutch were all fluent. There would be no need to worry. But she couldn't control a slight fluttering under her ribs. After buying mints and pocketing the change, she managed to work out how the lockers functioned and dumped her bag. Simple really, but she felt an exhilarating sense of achievement. She was ready to go.

She didn't know what to expect of Rotterdam. The major city in the Netherlands was Amsterdam, three hours drive away, and that was the place that got all the attention and publicity. She knew Rotterdam had been heavily bombed in the war and that was about it. Coming in on the coach from Europoort that morning, the heavily industrial approach had not been promising.

But now was the time to dig out the tourist leaflet she had picked up on the ferry. Lucky that she had. At least it could give her some idea. She nodded as she read, feeling more cheerful now. The city centre was better than she had expected. The best bits, according to the leaflet, were the Museum Park and the open-air maritime museum — or the old harbour on the Nieuwe Maas River. And some strangely-shaped dwellings called Cube Houses. But it didn't take her long to work out that she hadn't time to get to any of those. She didn't want to venture too far from the station where Danny would meet her. Eventually.

On her way to explore the very first pedestrianised shopping precinct in Europe, she noticed wide, straight streets and oddly-shaped modern buildings and abstract sculptures wherever you looked. The shopping centre, the Lijnbaan (pronounced Linebarn, the leaflet informed her helpfully) was fun, but small, and in no time she was through it and facing the old town hall, one of the very few old buildings that had escaped the bombing. She stood on the corner opposite and stared at the imposing mass of red brick and grey stone. Could you go in? Did they do conducted tours? It didn't look too likely. Probably it was only used for weddings and registering births, marriages and deaths. And the council offices.

Perhaps she should try to find that café after all. There was a chance that Danny might try to find her there if he finished early, wasn't there? She looked at her watch. All this had only taken her half an hour or so. What about a tourist office? Would that be in the town hall? Was it shown on her leaflet? Perhaps she could ask someone. She peered at the very basic sketch plan. Yes, there it was. Right next to where she was standing. She grinned. Lucky she hadn't asked. She would have looked like the typical foolish tourist. Although it was hardly surprising that she hadn't noticed as the large glass windows next to her seemed to suggest a well-stocked outdoor-pursuits shop. But, of course, that did make sense. Waterproofs and hiking gear would be useful purchases for tourists. And she could while away some time inside as well as getting a better map and some idea of where to go next. She rounded the corner onto a long straight street and once inside the building, finding someone to ask was easy.

'Here, madam.' The tall, thin assistant produced a much more detailed map and pointed. 'You are here, in Coolsingel.'

'Of course!' Emma rewarded him with such a dazzling smile that his eyes widened in surprise. She hadn't realised that Rotterdam would be so compact. Coolsingel was the second line of Danny's address. Well, since she was already so near, she might as well see if she could find it and have a look at his building from the outside. 'Wait a moment.' She fiddled in her wallet and produced the piece of paper with Danny's untidy scrawl. 'Can you tell me where this is?'

The assistant smiled back.

'Of course. Come.' He took her to the doorway and pointed. 'You can't miss it, as they say.'

Emma stared at the huge red brick apartment building in the distance and drew in her breath. It was as elegant as one of the modern sculptures. She should have expected the height, considering that the address showed her that Danny lived on the twenty seventh floor. She hadn't taken that in.

'Thank you. That's brilliant. How much do I owe you? For the map?'

He waved the money away.

'It is free. With the compliments of Mr van Lek. You will see his picture everywhere — he has given a great deal to the city.'

Mr van Lek's picture was certainly prominently displayed on his complimentary map. Emma glanced briefly at the smiling photograph. No doubt millionaire philanthropists had plenty to smile about, but he seemed exceptionally pleased with himself.

She thanked the assistant again and set off to stroll along the wide pavement. Perhaps by the time she got there, Danny would have finished 'seeing his people'. He would be surprised to hear that she was right outside. That would save time.

Except, she thought, as she paused beside the shopping mall at the foot of the building, craning her neck to look up, she didn't know where Danny's meeting would be taking place. It might even be near the station. She laughed again. It didn't matter. She estimated that the station was still only about ten minutes walk away if you went straight there.

She took out her phone again and stared at it. Should she ring him again? Surely he must have finished by now. Somehow, almost an hour had gone by. She frowned. Taken up with the new sights and sounds she had hardly noticed. A pity they had made this arrangement. She had his spare key, somewhere. Far better if she'd agreed to meet him inside. But she hadn't realised the flat would be so easy to find.

Her phone rang. Oh, good. There he was now.

'Hi, babe.' Always breezy and cheerful, that was Danny. 'Sorry about this. I won't be much longer now. Are you still at the station?'

What, after all this time? How entertaining would that have been?

Trust Danny not to think about that.

'No . . . Guess what, I'm looking up at your apartment block. Very impressive.'

'Oh, right.' He paused and she couldn't tell how he felt about that. She got the impression he was thinking quickly. 'Actually, that's good. Tell you what — you've got my spare key. Let yourself in and wait for me there. Help yourself to coffee. Make yourself at home. And make sure you collect the post on the way up. See you soon.'

'But — hang on!' Emma wasn't sure now whether the key was in the small backpack she was carrying, or in the larger bag back at the station. Too late, he'd gone. She frowned, trying to remember. Maybe she had left it in the bag with Danny's package? He hadn't even mentioned that. Didn't seem too bothered about it now. Which was odd considering all the fuss he'd made when he'd left it with her. She'd laughed and asked him why he didn't take it himself. There'd been some rushed and confusing explanation about the papers being confidential — lists of clients or something. Emma had wished she'd never asked.

At least she knew now that he wasn't intending to be long. She swung the small bag from her shoulders and rooted in the pockets. That was lucky. She remembered thinking that she wasn't going to need them, but had slid the spare keys in there all the same. Half-realising, no doubt, that knowing Danny, it was more than likely that she would need them. Two keys on the ring — obviously one for an outer door and one for the apartment.

* * *

She walked past the shopping mall and found the entrance lobby to the apartments round the back. The lobby had a number of postboxes against one wall. Yes, mustn't forget Danny's post, although she wondered why he hadn't bothered to collect it himself. But then, that was Danny all over. Why do anything yourself when you could get someone else to do it for you? The apartment key unlocked the box and there were several letters inside.

She scooped them up without looking at them, too busy working out where to go next. Ah, yes, the lift. She had a moment of doubt as she stepped into it, remembering the number of floors above her, but it shot up smoothly without any uncomfortable feeling of speed. An unremarkable landing, another door to unlock. However, once she was inside, Emma was on top of the world.

Vast windows formed two sides of a triangular space in the sitting room. Light and blue sky and clouds and the tops of the few buildings that equalled this one in height. Mostly silvery-grey glass and sculptural shapes. She took a deep breath, immediately loving the flat and the view.

A small kitchen was half concealed in one corner, and beyond that there were two bedrooms — one also with windows on two sides — a bathroom, a short corridor, and you were back to the entrance door. The flat was small, but spacious and modern with the minimum of furniture.

She was blown away, floating up here in the clouds. Nothing Danny had said had prepared her for this. All his business deals must be going incredibly well.

Perhaps leaving her bag at the station had been a bad move; she would have been able to unpack now. But retrieving it wouldn't take long. She did as Danny had suggested — helped herself to a coffee and sat down on one of the wide, low sills to drink in the view. Usually she wasn't too keen on heights, but here she was so far up that it didn't bother her. If that made any sense.

From here she could see the street below clearly: tiny cars, bicycles, minuscule figures and all in two directions. She might even be able to see Danny approaching. She smiled at the idea of seeing him before he could see her.

And, yes — even as she formed the thought, here he was now. Striding along, head down, in his hurried, familiar way. *Look up*, she thought, ready to wave, *look up here*. Silly — even if he did, he wouldn't be able to see her. There was no chance of him picking her out amongst the wall of anonymous windows. Yes, he was pausing, turning his head — but no, only to look over his shoulder. He was rounding the corner, disappearing from view, obviously making his way to the entrance. He would be here in a minute, assuming the lift was free. She was within sight of the front door from her vantage point, so she stayed where she was.

Just as she turned to face the door, an unusual movement in the street below caught her eye as a small car swept up onto the pavement. Emma leaned forward, surprised.

Surely that wasn't allowed. There had been no sign of any illegal parking during her walk that morning. At any minute surely the Dutch traffic wardens would be swarming around — if they had traffic wardens here. Now two men were jumping out, both wearing long dark coats in spite of the heat, slamming the doors behind them and it seemed, running towards where the entrance to the block must be.

Were they the police? Was someone being arrested? Danny might see them on his way up. If not, he would be surprised when she told him. She faced the door squarely now, but still paid attention to the street below, glancing down and waiting for further developments. Danny would be sorry to have missed all the excitement.

Surely, though, Danny was taking a long time? Even if someone else had been using the lift. Where was he? Now the men were back at the car. The arrest hadn't taken long. If it had been an arrest.

Maybe they had just come to collect a friend. In a hurry. Because there were three figures now and the third man didn't seem well because the others were supporting him. Head down and almost covered by another dark coat. It must be an arrest, then. How odd. Surely Danny must have seen them. Perhaps he would know the ailing third man. And where was he . . . ?

* * *

Later, Emma realised that she had avoided the conclusion that had been staring her in the face because she just didn't want to believe it. She watched the car swerve away, narrowly missing two pedestrians and a cyclist to rejoin the traffic. And it was gone.

Emma sat very still, her body feeling like one huge heartbeat. Slowly she turned her head to gaze at the front door once more.

Perhaps she had been mistaken. Perhaps it had not been Danny striding confidently towards the entrance. She was so high up here that everything below was far away and foreshortened.

There would be dozens of people dressed in a dark t-shirt and jeans. And with similar hair, dark and untidy.

She was almost convincing herself now. Almost, but not quite. Keep going. Even if it *had* been Danny, he might have popped into one of the other flats on the way up. He must know people here. And, of course — this was easily solved. She could ring him. She reached for her phone and pressed Danny's number, realising that she was holding her breath as it rang. The ringing stopped.

'Hello?' she said. There was no answering voice, only a living breathing silence. 'Danny? Are you there?' Abruptly, even the breathing noises were gone — as if Danny had switched off. But why would he do that?

She took a deep, shaky breath herself. Now what? She stood up and began pacing up and down, hugging herself as if the room had suddenly become cold. She couldn't just sit up here. Not now. She had to do something. She must go out and look around for him. If Danny wanted to know where she was, he could ring her.

Carefully, she locked the door behind her and summoned the lift. As before, there was no sign of anyone on the landing — but there were only two flats on each floor. No sign of anyone at ground level, either, but she knew that the apartments would be occupied mainly by young professionals. By this time — mid-morning on a week day — they would be at work in their various offices.

She walked out onto the street, looking upwards. Looked round. This was getting her nowhere. At least back in the apartment she had a safe base with food and drink on hand. Or she assumed that she had; she must check Danny's fridge. She was suddenly ravenously hungry — surely in one of these shops there must be somewhere she could get a sandwich?

Yes, there was. She found one with pre-packed snacks and a choice of ham and cheese sandwiches in various combinations. Cheese with ham. Ham with cheese. A large amount of cheese with just a little ham. A large amount of ham . . . *Stop that*, Emma told herself firmly. What would the girl behind the till do if she suddenly shouted, 'Please help me, I think my boyfriend's been kidnapped?' Well, she had no intention of finding out. She was going to tackle this sensibly. She smiled at the girl and the success of making her transaction with another note calmed her a little. She was worrying needlessly. Danny would be back by now and wondering where she was.

There was still no sign of anyone in the anonymous cream painted entrance hall. She was getting used to that by now. Stepped into the lift and pressed number twenty seven. Not far from the top. There were thirty-two floors altogether.

Emma moved backwards idly and felt something beneath her foot. She looked down and frowned as she picked it up, recognising the silvery plastic pound sign from Danny's own key ring. A silly thing she had given him herself, so there was no mistaking it. It couldn't have fallen off so easily, surely? A shiver of unease flicked across her shoulder blades. What had happened here? A struggle? The reflective metallic walls in the lift gave no further clues.

She was glancing at the other front door on the shared landing. Who lived there? Might they have seen or heard anything? She tried the bell but there was no answer. No, this was silly. He would be back in the flat by now. In a minute or two, they would be laughing at her fears. Danny would be waiting — or hiding in the kitchen ready to leap out shouting 'Surprise!' It would be just like him. Or the bathroom? She unlocked the front door quickly, almost convincing herself.

No. And now she had completed the full circle of the flat and was back at the front door. She felt like flinging herself down on the huge cream coloured corner sofa and letting the tears come because she sensed they weren't far away.

But that wouldn't help. Better to sit down, eat her ham and cheese and decide carefully and calmly what to do next. She forced herself to keep chewing each mouthful, slowly and deliberately, making it last. In spite of her hunger she was hardly noticing what she was eating. She placed the sandwich packet in the bin, wiped the crumbs from the table — and behind her heard a key being inserted into the lock . . .

2

Emma opened her mouth to welcome Danny with a joyful shout, but the sound died before she uttered it. Something about the slow, careful, even secretive way the key was being handled.

It couldn't be Danny. He didn't do anything slowly or carefully. She backed away. Looking round instinctively for something to defend herself with. There was only a potted plant with dark spiky leaves. She held it in front of her, wishing she had thought to dodge into the kitchen instead. Too late now.

The door opened. She saw a man with broad shoulders, a handsome, open face and fair hair. No one she recognised. He froze when he saw her.

'Who are you? What are you doing here?'

She found her voice although her mouth was dry.

'I could ask the same thing. What are you doing here?' She must look stupid, clutching her plant but she didn't feel like putting it down.

'Er — I'm the landlord.'

Emma frowned cautiously, trying to remember the landlord's name. Danny had mentioned him once, hadn't he? There had been some disagreement when the washing machine had broken down. 'I see.'

He smiled easily.

'Well, you could say that I'm here on the landlord's behalf.'

'Right.'

'Danny asked me to pop in and check a few things. Needing repair, you know?'

'He didn't mention it. And the washer's fine now, thanks.'

'It's a routine thing. Mr van der Tholen likes to check the inventory every six months. I thought Danny was out. I must apologise. I would have rung the bell if I'd known you were here.'

Yes. Van der Tholen. That was the name she'd been struggling for. This person knew the landlord's name and he had a key. So he must be okay, mustn't he? She managed a smile though she could still feel her heart thumping loudly in her chest.

'I'm Danny's girlfriend. Emma Ash-croft. I'm staying with him for a few days.'

He nodded.

'Pleased to meet you. Well, I'll have a quick look round if that's okay.'

He was moving around the sitting room without waiting for an answer, eyes alert. Certainly looked as if he were checking something. But surely he should have brought the inventory with him?

She replaced the plant and followed him through the house.

'And you are?'

'Ah — Steven.' Didn't seem to be volunteering a surname.

'Your English is very good.'

He smiled without looking at her.

'I am English.' He was opening and shutting drawers now, checking the kitchen cupboards. 'But you must be busy. Don't let me interrupt you.'

Emma wasn't going to leave him to do this on his own.

'Don't you have to tick things off? What are you going to do if you find anything?'

'What? Oh — I know what to look for. I do these inspections a lot. Didn't you bring any luggage?'

The abrupt question threw her for a moment.

'I left my bag at the station. When Danny turns up, we can go and collect it.' And this had absolutely nothing to do with him. She felt annoyed with herself for volunteering the information.

He was still looking at her, cryptically. And almost as if he didn't believe her at all.

'I only got here today,' she said

defensively. 'I haven't even seen Danny yet. Not that it has anything to do with you.'

'You haven't?' He was back in the sitting room, shuffling through the letters she had placed on the dining table.

'That's Danny's post,' she said sharply. 'You don't have to go through that.'

'There's one for you.'

'What? How can there be? No one would be writing to me here.'

'Delivered by hand,' he said, passing it to her. Of course. Danny's writing. She felt an overwhelming relief. No doubt this letter would explain everything. No wonder Danny had asked her to collect the post. But why hadn't he left the note in the flat? 'Aren't you going to open it?' Steven asked.

She slid it into the pocket of her jeans. Not yet. No way. Not with those cool blue eyes appraising her so sharply.

'Well, thank you, Mr — Steven. If

you've seen all you need to see, I'll show you out.'

'When did you last speak to Danny?'

'About half an hour ago,' Emma said reluctantly. She looked at her watch. 'More than that now.'

'Did he seem okay?'

She hesitated. Somehow she sensed that a great deal could depend on how she reacted to this simple question.

She was very much on her own here, in a strange city. And Danny's letter couldn't possibly explain everything; he must have written it before he was bundled away.

She had to be realistic and accept that something terrible had happened to Danny. And she needed to talk to someone. More than anything, she wanted to run through what she had witnessed and find out whether she was over-reacting.

And Steven was English and knew the landlord. And he was all she'd got. If he'd lived in Rotterdam for a while, at least he'd be able to advise her on what to do next.

He was still waiting for an answer to his question but without hassling her. Standing in front of her with a contained patience, giving her time. As if he was waiting for her to work it out.

She took a deep breath.

'No, not really. I'm not sure. Perhaps you'd better sit down for a minute.' She sat down too, positioning herself on one of the dining chairs facing him. 'So — here goes.' Telling him everything, from her arrival at the station took less than five minutes, even when he had questioned her closely on exactly what she had seen and what Danny had said. There was so little to go on. 'I'm so very much afraid that something bad has happened to him.' She sat back, hoping for the incredulous laughter that would make everything okay.

He didn't laugh. His face was more serious than ever.

'I'm afraid I agree with you. And also, whoever those people are, I don't think they'll be leaving it there.'

'What do you mean?'

'It seems to me that Danny could have something they want. And if he can't produce it for them, whatever it is — they may well come back here. I think you should get out of here, Emma. Now.' He rose to his feet.

Emma sat where she was, unable to move. Her spine felt rigid.

'I don't believe I'm hearing this.' She looked out of the high windows and yes, the memorable skyline was still there and way below the ants were still scurrying about in the street, just as usual. Nothing had changed. There was no sign of that small car and those sinister looking men. But was Steven right? Would they be coming back?

His voice was urgent.

'We have to leave.' He took her elbow and pulled her to her feet.

'But how can I? I haven't anywhere to go. And if I stay here, Danny can find me when he comes back. That's what I need to do.'

'If he comes back. And if he does, he

may not be the only one. There may be other interested parties coming here.'

'But why would they be interested in me?'

'I don't suppose they would be. But if Danny doesn't prove helpful to them, they may well be interested in searching the flat. And I wouldn't advise you to be here when they arrive.'

Emma stared at him, her brain suddenly functioning at full speed.

'Hey, hang on. That's what you were doing, isn't it? Searching the flat? I wondered why you didn't have any kind of checklist. Repairs indeed.' She pulled her arm away. 'Okay, I'm leaving. But what makes you think I'm leaving with you? I'll look after myself, thanks.' She thought, I'll go back to the Tourist Office and ask about finding a hotel. But first I'll go to the police and report Danny missing.

He shrugged.

'Whatever you say. Just as long as we both get out of here.'

Emma snatched up her backpack and

jacket and made her way towards the door. She didn't bother to look round to see if Steven was following. But of course, he was.

She almost paused before stepping into the lift. Could she trust him? Was being alone in the lift with him a good idea? But if he had wanted to harm her, he would have had every opportunity inside the flat. All the same, it seemed better if she kept her doubts to herself for now. She reached out for the ground floor button and his hand was there first, pressing for the first floor.

'We'll get out there and send it on to the ground without us.'

'Why?'

'Think about it. When the lift doors open, we don't know who or what we may see. And we'd have nowhere to run.'

Emma nodded.

'Okay.' She could see the point of that, she supposed. Although she wasn't certain that behaving in such a complicated way was really necessary.

She followed him out of the lift onto the first floor landing and down the stairs. The way he was looking this way and that was getting to her now, making her feel jumpy. There was no need for his restraining arm as they reached the ground floor.

No way would she be dashing out into the hallway without looking. They peered round the corner and Emma began to breathe a sigh of relief at the sight of the lift waiting harmlessly, doors open. A relief at once quashed as the sunlight at the glass exit doors was obscured by two dark shadows. She swallowed, her mouth dry and painful.

Even after only seeing them from above and so briefly, she recognised the two men. Close up, they seemed huge. Smartly dressed in immaculate dark suits and black macks but with heavy shoulders and cold eyes. No way could Danny have evaded them. Hardly pausing, the men used a key and came straight through into the lobby.

Emma's heart lurched. If she had not

already been hanging onto the wall, she would have swayed and fallen. Her throat was dry with fear. Thank goodness that the give-away number twenty-seven was no longer showing on the floors panel. Only number one was lit up and that told them nothing. They stepped inside and the lift doors closed behind them.

'It's okay,' Steven said, as if reading her mind. 'They may not know about you. Yet. And when Danny does tell them, they won't necessarily know what you look like.'

'You mean, if he tells them.' Surely Danny wouldn't put her into danger so quickly? But her voice emerged as a terrified squeak.

'Okay, if. Still, it's high time we got out of here.'

Emma didn't need urging. She was running after him in a blind panic. Unable to breathe freely or think straight, her only need was to get as far away as possible before the two men in dark suits came down again. They turned several corners until Emma had no idea where she was.

'Hey, wait,' she gasped. 'Where are we going?'

Okay, she was away from one danger but she had no intention of diving straight into another. Her brain was beginning to work again. There were too many holes in Steven's story for her liking. *I have to get back to the tourist office*, she thought. It was the only safe haven she could think of. But some instinct told her she should keep this to herself.

Steven stopped.

'Flight over for now. Best that we look casual.' He took off his distinctive tan-coloured jacket and slung it over one arm with only the nondescript beige coloured lining showing. He turned, saw her expression and grinned. 'Yes, I know. It's hideous isn't it? But instantly recognisable. As soon as I take it off, people have absolutely no idea at all whether they saw me or not.'

'Brilliant.' Emma nodded. At the

same time, she was thinking that she wouldn't forget his face so quickly. There was something about him . . . They sauntered around yet another corner and Steven steered her to a nearby pavement café. 'Time to regroup. Coffee? I'll get them.'

Time to make a stand. She looked up at him, ignoring the chair he was pointing to.

'I think I should go to the police.'

He nodded, seemingly untroubled by this suggestion.

'We'll talk about that. Coffee first.' He slung the jacket over one of the chairs on the pavement and disappeared into the café. She sat down. He'd dumped the jacket carelessly or so it had seemed — but only the dull-coloured lining remained visible all the same.

Had that been deliberate? Perhaps he had done this kind of thing before. Perhaps Mr Steven whoever-he-was could do with answering a few questions before they went any further with this. If they did. Yes, he had got her out of a sticky situation just now and she was grateful but she still wasn't certain whether to trust him or not.

For a few minutes, she could see his back through the large window and then as the queue moved forward, he was out of sight. That meant that she would be invisible to him, too.

She could run. Now. Would she ever have a better chance? But he would be after her before she had covered ten yards and she was suddenly aware that her legs felt heavy and weak. She hadn't slept well on the ferry and had been up to be ready to disembark since 6am. So she wasn't sure how much energy she could summon up and also she would be running through a city she didn't know. At present, all the advantages were with Steven. She would have to engineer a situation where she would have a better opportunity and more time.

Her eyes were drawn to his jacket. In concealing the distinctive orangey-tan colour, he had displayed his inside pockets. Foolish. You never knew who could be watching, ready to seize the opportunity. No point in evading the kidnappers and laying yourself open to every passing pickpocket.

She reached out, only intending to re-arrange the sleeves somehow. Yes, now she could see a wallet — or something like that. Careless.

An idea struck her. Perhaps she could just have a quick look inside. Because if there was an identity card, that would verify whether he was who he said he was.

She stood up and pretended to stretch her arms while glancing towards the café. Not a very convincing reason for standing where she could see him but it would have to do. And he wasn't looking this way so it was all right. Yes, Steven was moving forwards towards the counter, but there were still two or three people in front of him.

She sat down quickly. There would be time for a quick glimpse. Her hands were shaking. *No*, she thought, *I can't do this*. But it was the only way she could find out whether she could trust him. And she wasn't going to take anything.

She put her backpack on the table, leaned forward as if looking inside it and slid the slim black plastic wallet out of Steven's pocket.

She opened it — and thrust it straight back as if it were red hot. A stupid reaction but only because she was so surprised. He was a policeman. Not based here in Holland but somewhere in the UK. She wished she had given herself a longer look and read it properly. But she had seen enough. Just in time because here he was now.

'Hope you're okay with milk.'

She clutched her bag towards her, moving it off the table and certain she was turning bright red. Guilt must be written all over her. She wasn't cut out for this. But he didn't seem to have noticed anything.

'Thanks. Just what I need,' she said.

'And thank you for getting me out of that. It could have been a nasty situation.' She was gabbling. Calm down, she told herself.

He pushed his jacket aside without looking at it and sat down.

'You might have been well on the way to finding out where Danny is by now. If I hadn't intervened. They could have grabbed you too and your questions would all be answered — but not in a way you would like.'

Emma hadn't thought of that. So much new information was being thrust at her that she couldn't make sense of it all.

'Oh — you mean, they would have captured me and taken me to wherever they're holding Danny?' She shivered. 'I'm sure you're right.'

'So, what next? Time to find out what's in Danny's letter, don't you think?' He was smiling at her in a disturbingly lazy way that gave the impression he knew all her thoughts and was inwardly laughing. It could have been annoying, but surprisingly wasn't.

The immediate danger was over, thanks to him, and she was beginning to feel reassured by his calm. And if he was with the British police, she knew she could trust him. Although why would a British policeman be interested in Danny? Because they had found out that he was in danger and might need protection maybe? She hoped that was all it was.

'The letter,' he said gently.

'Sorry.' She managed a shaky smile as she took the envelope out of her pocket, holding it towards herself. 'If you don't mind, it could be personal.' But he was making no attempt to lean forward or twist round to see what Danny had written. He trusted her. And she had repaid that trust by rooting in his pockets.

She felt her face growing hot again. Quickly, she tore the envelope open. There was only one sheet of paper, covered in Danny's large scrawl.

Just in case I don't catch up with you this morning, I'll see you in Delft, three to four Dutch time this afternoon. Café with yellow chairs on the Beast market. D. PS Bring Dough Woman with you. Loads of it for us. Cheers.

She couldn't help grinning, although not having the faintest idea of what he meant. That was so like Danny, The whole thing was like Danny; she could just hear him saying the words, throwing them over his shoulder at her as he dashed off yet again.

'Good news?' Steven asked quietly.

'Oh — yes. At least I know where to go next.' She folded the paper in half, concealing the message. Decision time. Should she thank him for his help and leave? She had no guarantee that he wouldn't follow her anyway.

He might get in touch with the police in Delft and she would find them waiting for her. Would that be helpful to Danny or not? It might even make things worse. If she stuck with Steven, at least she would know what he was doing.

Okay, she thought, she might as well trust him. For the moment. 'I'm to meet Danny in Delft this afternoon. Before four o'clock.'

He looked at his watch.

'I can give you a lift there, if you like,' he suggested. 'No problem.'

'Thanks.' But what about the rest of the message? And considering what she had witnessed from the flat, would Danny even be able to make this appointment? He'd written the note before being abducted. But she had no other leads. And he might get away from those people somehow. She looked directly at Steven, trying to read his reaction. 'I still think I should go to the police. I don't know what's happened to Danny.'

'No need.' He felt for his jacket and produced the identity card she had seen already. 'I am the police.'

'Oh. Good.' Emma blushed, trying to look surprised. 'Yes, that's great.'

'We're liaising indirectly with the police in Rotterdam on this operation, but it would only confuse things if you tried to involve them at a local level.'

She was only too conscious of the folded letter in her hand. If only Danny had managed to write something that made sense. She straightened her shoulders.

'I need to know why. And what operation? Why are you interested in Danny?'

3

He didn't answer straightaway. He sipped his coffee with that smiling intent stare, as if he were weighing her up. She found herself thinking . . . *If I wasn't going out with Danny . . . No. Don't go there* . . . before remembering with a jolt of surprise that soon she might not be Danny's girlfriend. She had forgotten the underlying purpose of her visit and the decision she had intended to make. But now, with her concern for Danny's safety over-riding her other feelings, she wasn't sure how she felt. She was even more confused than before.

'How long have you known Danny?' he asked.

'Oh — almost a year now.'

She might have added, 'Off and on. Coming and going.' Sometimes it felt as though Danny had been absent more often than he had been present. If you calculated the time that she had actually spent with him, it could probably be counted only in weeks. Perhaps even days.

'And you and he — is this a long-term, serious relationship?'

When her mother had asked the same thing, Emma had bitten her head off. Somehow she didn't mind Steven asking. She must just stop analysing her feelings so much, she told herself. Go with the flow. She smiled.

'I thought so, at one point. Danny's so exciting to be with. Everything is fun.' She sighed. 'I'm no longer sure whether that's enough. I actually came over here to sort out how I feel about him.' There. She had said the words out loud. They were official. She laughed, although she didn't feel much like laughing considering how the visit was turning out. It must have been a nervous reaction. How like Danny to turn all her plans upside down, intentionally or not.

'I need to ask you,' she began abruptly. 'Though I'm not sure whether I really want to hear the answer. Are you trying to protect Danny — or to investigate him?'

Steven leaned forward, resting his arms on the table. His hands were within centimetres of the letter, although he gave no sign of having noticed.

'Maybe both. We have to protect him in order to investigate him. Not much point in following up on an investigation if the subject is no longer available.'

'Oh, no,' Emma gasped. 'You mean — something bad might have happened to him?' She stared at Steven, feeling cold. Not wanting to voice the unspeakable, but unable to stop the words coming out. 'You don't mean that he might even be dead?'

'No. Don't think that.' He shook his head, reaching out to touch her hand. 'I didn't mean that at all.' There seemed to be genuine regret in his voice. 'I'm sorry — I shouldn't have put it like that. I was well out of order.'

'Are you sure?' Emma said weakly. He was still touching her hand reassuringly. In spite of that moment of horror, she was aware of the warmth of his hand over hers.

'Absolutely. I'm certain Danny is far too valuable to them alive. So you don't need to worry about that.' Slowly, as if he hardly noticed what he was doing, he moved his hand back to the table. 'And I can't prove anything about Danny's activities — not yet. But it seems from what we've seen today that he is certainly in with some very dodgy individuals. And could get his fingers burned.'

'I can't believe I'm hearing this.' Emma put a hand to her mouth. Not fun loving Danny. He was too open — too disorganised, even — to be successful at anything criminal. Wasn't he? But already Steven had proved to her that Danny had obviously got himself involved with something that was probably criminal — or he knew men who certainly were.

And he could have thoughtlessly laid Emma open to goodness knows what dangers. She had to admit it to herself now. Yes, she had to believe that of him. She took a deep breath, making an instinctive decision.

'You'd better see the note.' She pushed it towards him.

He opened it without altering his position and yet she was at once aware that all his senses had become alert. There was a different tone in his voice.

'So what does this last bit mean?'

'I've absolutely no idea,' Emma admitted, shrugging her shoulders.

'Are you sure? He sounds as if he expects you to understand.'

She stared back at him.

'Of course I'm sure.' It was as if the good-humoured link between them had been severed. What had happened? He obviously didn't believe her. Was he thinking that she was involved in Danny's supposed criminal activities, whatever they were?

His voice was brisk rather than friendly.

'What did Danny do exactly? To make a living?'

Not an easy question to answer when she wasn't sure herself. She blushed, wishing she had something more definite to tell him.

'He travelled about a lot. Europe mostly. He was a free agent specialising in financial trouble shooting. People approached him when they had a problem.'

There was no trace now of the easy smile. The blue eyes were cold. As if he didn't believe a word of it.

'He said he wanted to relax when he was out with me. He said talking about work was boring.' Emma leaned forward. 'How often do *you* discuss your work with your girlfriend — or wife?'

'Not a problem. I don't have either.'

A little ping of delight registered inside her head. She brushed it aside, almost crossly.

'You know what I mean. If you had one.'

He ignored the comment.

'I'm wondering if any of these firms who sought his help had an interest in the art world. Paintings? Antiques?'

'I've just told you. He never talked about work.' She stopped, too abruptly to be able to pretend. 'Oh. Well — he may have been interested in the last few weeks. But nothing to do with work. He was talking about collecting paintings as an investment. When he had some spare cash.'

'And you didn't think that was odd?'

'Why on earth should I?' But yes, she had thought so. She'd teased him about it. He'd laughed and said, 'Just you wait, babe. When I'm an international art collector — with art thieves stealing to order for me, we'll see who has the last laugh.' No way was she telling Steven that one. It had been one of Danny's jokes. Obviously. The kind of wild thing he said all the time. She wriggled uncomfortably in her seat, wishing that Steven didn't give her the feeling he was reading her mind.

'We had a laugh about it,' she said defensively. 'I said, where was he going to keep them and were we going to start visiting art galleries? He said, no need, he could do all that on the internet.'

'Was he interested in any artist in particular?'

Emma tried to remember. Watching Danny's computer screens flickering past had made her dizzy. He surfed as quickly as he did everything else.

'Anyone in fashion. Any artist whose work is selling well at present. And, oh, yes — in particular, any artists who might have paintings that have never been found. There could be records of actual paintings being completed that have never been seen since or gaps in the work they did that can't be properly accounted for. They may have given work away to pay for the next meal or the rent or something. And now worth millions.'

'Go on.'

'I don't know — Monet, Van Gogh. Two big names. But he gave up on those two pretty quickly.' She remembered Danny flashing through screen after screen of small seventeenth century domestic interiors. *Woman with Jug of Milk. Girl with a Pearl Earring*. She said, 'Vermeer, I think.' She looked up at Steven's face and down at the note. 'Was it possible that this Dough Woman could be a painting?'

His voice was deceptively pleasant.

'And you're telling me you've only just realised that?' She squirmed under the flash of disbelief in his eyes.

'You're not getting it,' she said defensively. 'Danny was interested in all kinds of things. Anything that might have money in it. He got excited about a new kind of soap powder once. And he had an idea about finding people who'd invented things and didn't know how to take it further. There was a mass of info he printed out on how soap functions. Vermeer kind of got lost in the bubbles. And you can believe me or not, but that's the truth.'

* * *

She didn't feel she could cope with the mix of emotions. Suddenly, she could believe only too well that Danny had been mixed up in something shady. How could she have been so blind? Because she'd wanted to love Danny, she supposed. Assuming she could believe Steven. She was beginning to wonder how well she could trust anyone. Obviously she was a hopeless judge of character. She felt foolish and betrayed. She reached for the note and crumpled it up in her hands.

'Hey, that's evidence.' Steven took it from her hand and smoothed it out.

Emma hardly noticed. Her heart was beating wildly. What about the package in her luggage? Surely it was too small to be a painting? No, it wasn't. Not if it had been taken from its frame.

Had Danny had her travelling carelessly on the ferry and the coach with an undiscovered Vermeer? She shivered. She had left that bag all over the place, without thinking about it. And where might Danny have obtained the painting from in the first place?

'You've just thought of something. I think you had better share it with me.' His voice was grim.

No point in denying it. Steven would be too close to piecing it together as it was. She told him in a low voice, feeling unutterably stupid.

'I should have realised. I should have thought. I was just trying to be helpful. He said it was paperwork. It felt as if it could be. I didn't have any reason to think it wasn't.' She lifted her head. 'We'd better get down to the railway station and get it back, hadn't we? Then we can hand it to the police.'

He considered this only for a moment or two.

'No. I think it's safer where it is. For now. What we need to do is get you to your appointment with Danny.'

'Sorry?' Emma stared at him. This seemed a very strange plan.

'Danny is expecting you to hand it

over. This way, he'll probably be annoyed if you turn up without it, but he won't suspect anything. And if you give him the locker key instead, I can arrange for him to be picked up as he collects it. We can't do much unless we get him with the painting in his possession.'

Yes, that did make sense. Emma nodded.

'But we don't even know that we're right and the package is this painting. Shouldn't we go and have a look and put it back?'

'Not a very safe option. How certain are we that we aren't being followed?'

Emma shivered. 'You mean — someone could be watching us now?'

He placed a warning hand over hers. 'Don't look round, just in case. We have to appear perfectly natural at all times.' His hand was warm and strong. Again, she felt a flicker of regret when he removed it. She was glad Steven was here. In this whole horrible and confusing mess, he was the one bright aspect of the situation. If only they could return to that easy friendliness that had been developing. Surely he believed her now and she had dissolved those moments of distrust?

The thought of unknown pursuers out there somewhere was frightening and disturbing. What would they do to her if they found her? What were they doing to Danny?

'Who are these people?' Her voice was tight with fear.

'We're not certain. That's what we want to find out. And why it's so important for you to keep this appointment. It's the only lead we have.' He leaned forward again, his face serious. 'But only if you're okay with this. You don't have to do it.'

She felt that she was almost drowning in the cool eyes. Except that now they were warm and pleading. Refusing was not an option. She wanted to help.

'Yes,' she said. 'I'll do it.'

4

Steven smiled at her. 'Good.' He stood up. 'So suddenly we have time on our hands. How about something to eat?'

'Great idea.' The ham and cheese sandwich seemed a very long time ago, although everything had happened so fast; surely it couldn't have been long enough for her to be feeling this hungry. The tension that had tied steel bands around her midriff since she had looked down from the windows in the flat seemed to be lessening a little.

That distant sandwich had stood in for breakfast and now she was starving. All the excitement and the hurrying about, she supposed. That sandwich must have been — how long ago? She looked at her watch and exclaimed in surprise. Well over an hour.

'Here?' she asked, but already Steven was moving away from the café.

'I don't think so. A bit too close to our starting point. No point in hanging around now that we've decided what we're doing.'

'Yes, of course.' Emma frowned. 'They're still looking for us.'

'Do you mind if I put my arm round your shoulders?' He was scanning the street as they walked and didn't wait for her answer. Emma was conscious of how close they were now.

She felt the tension building all over again but for a very different reason. Steven laughed. 'Relax, it's okay. This is only a precaution. If they're looking for anyone, it will be for a girl on her own. Not a couple.'

'Sorry.' Emma was annoyed with herself for giving her feelings away. 'I'm not usually this jittery.'

'Nothing to be sorry for. Anyone would be.'

Emma had hardly noticed where they were going. They were twisting and turning in a maze of small back streets. She glimpsed patches of graffiti and boarded windows. Was this a good idea? But even as the unwelcome thought formed, a final corner brought them within view of a busier street.

'In here,' Steven said and she realised he was guiding her through a red-painted doorway into a small entrance hall. Stairs led upwards. She thought wildly, what is this? Was this where Steven lived? Made sense if they needed to hide. Perhaps he was going to get a takeaway. Or cook something. But she didn't know how she would feel about being on her own with him for the next couple of hours.

'Don't stop here,' Steven said. 'We'll look at the menu upstairs.'

Emma felt her face growing hot. Of course, the menu on the wall and the large potted plant were a bit of a giveaway. Wishful thinking, maybe. Well, she must stop that. Concentrate on what they were doing. Never mind that she was with one of the most fanciable men she had ever come across.

'This is a Chinese restaurant?' Trying to cover her confusion, she had only made things worse. Of course it was. Only an idiot would think that Holland was only windmills and clogs and tulips.

'Indonesian. The Dutch have many historic links with the Far East. They were always great seafarers and traders.'

'Yes, yes of course. The Dutch East Indies and all that.' Once up the stairs they entered a room containing about twenty tables, laid with spotless white cloths and gleaming cutlery.

Steven spoke to the waiter in fluent Dutch and they were led over to a corner table where the large windows were on two sides. Steven pulled out a chair for her and seated himself with a good view of the street, Emma noticed. She shivered a little. To disguise her reaction, she said, 'Your Dutch is very good.'

He brushed her compliment away.

'Oh — I went to an evening class. I need to practice. I gather my accent isn't that great. Now, I can recommend the Chicken Satay, a great favourite in the Netherlands if you want something typically Dutch. And they do a particularly good one here.'

'That's fine.' Emma didn't mind what she had.

'Best that we keep to something fairly light. Not too filling.' He added, 'And quick.'

'I thought we had plenty of time. Is it far to Delft?'

'We do. And no, it isn't far at all. But some eating places over here can be painfully slow. That other café, for instance. Excellent food, leisurely service.'

'Okay.' Emma was happy to take his word for it. She was still reading the menu, enjoying the unfamiliar phrases. 'What's this one? Something *tafel*?'

'You've gone straight for the best there.' He smiled. 'It translates as 'rice table'. A selection of everything they do. Always a good choice in Holland. We haven't time to do it justice now. Tell you what, I'd very much like to treat you to one later.' He stopped. His voice became more formal. 'Sorry. I was out of order there. Forget I said anything. You're in a relationship.'

'Not really,' Emma sighed. 'Not any more. I thought I'd explained.'

'You did.' Steven paused. 'But Danny doesn't know that yet, does he? So it's probably not such a good idea. We'll see how everything works out.'

'Fair enough.' She nodded, but she was disappointed. There had been a brief flash of warmth in his eyes, hadn't there?

'Yes,' she said finally. 'I have a lot of sorting to do. And I will.' And now she was almost resenting Danny which was wrong when she didn't know what had happened to him. She felt a niggling wave of remorse.

Steven was right; the service was swift and efficient and the chicken satay was very good. She tried to concentrate on her food, staring down at her plate, rather than meeting the perceptive blue eyes.

'So tell me about yourself,' he said. 'Where do you live in the UK?'

She welcomed his innocuous question with relief and found herself telling him all about her mum in Leeds and her disapproving sisters and her job in an insurance office.

How she'd made a mistake in taking that direction, but she knew how lucky she was to have a job these days.

His questions were cleverly designed to get her talking, she suspected, and he seemed genuinely interested. At last she seized the opportunity, hardly taking a breath at the end of a sentence.

'But what about you? That's enough about me for now.'

Steven put down his knife and fork and took a drink of water. That could almost have been a signal because immediately the softly-spoken waiter was beside them, murmuring urgently. Steven took a note out of his wallet and pressed it into the waiter's hand, giving a gesture that Emma took to mean he didn't want any change.

'Emma? We have to go. I'm sorry.'

* * *

She had a dozen questions to ask, but sensing his urgency, merely nodded and collected her bag and jacket. Now the waiter was ushering them away from the stairs, through the doorway and into the kitchen.

Emma gained a fleeting impression of stainless steel and hot steaming pans before they were going down a narrow stairway and out onto a street she didn't recognise. In moments, however, they were crossing the main street she had glimpsed as they arrived at the restaurant. Only briefly before plunging into another alleyway and crossing another shopping street. Almost running but not quite; that would have made them too conspicuous, Emma guessed.

'I thought we were safe there,' she gasped.

'We were. We got away, didn't we?'

'So were they following us, all that time?'

'I doubt it. I think they got lucky.'

Suddenly, Steven pulled her into a vacant shop doorway and was kissing her. Bemused, she found herself kissing him back. And besides, she realised joyfully, she wanted to kiss him back. He released her gently and she staggered a little. Her legs were feeling weak and her heart was racing.

'Sorry about that,' he was saying. 'I didn't want them to see you before we go down into the car park. It's okay now. They've gone.'

She hadn't seen them. She only had Steven's word that they had been there at all. Perhaps, Emma thought hopefully, he might have made the whole thing up. As an excuse. But, no, he had made it clear that he wanted to be fair to Danny. It had been a purely professional kiss.

All the same, she felt as though she was floating. That kiss may not have been a good idea if he wanted her to function like an intelligent being. She stepped into the small car beside him and tried to think sobering thoughts. She was relieved to find that this wasn't too difficult given the circumstances.

* * *

Steven was right; the drive to Delft didn't take long. Now she was wishing that Delft had been further away. She wasn't looking forward to this part of it. Perhaps they would have a long walk to the meeting place? But they found the Beastmarket — or the Beestenmarkt — without trouble. Here, as in Rotterdam, Steven seemed to know his way around.

She had been doubtful about Danny's directions. A café with yellow chairs? But it was easy. The Beestenmarkt, a shady cobbled square, was filled with seating areas belonging to the surrounding cafés — all identified by the colour of the chairs and tables. She was about to step away from the crowds on the pavement, assuming that Steven would follow, when he touched her arm gently.

'You'd better go and sit down on your own.'

Occupied with the relief of deciphering Danny's directions, she hadn't thought about what was going to happen at this meeting. Her stomach dropped.

'Don't worry. I'll be in sight at all times. I'll stand by that doorway. Tell Danny the bag was too heavy to bring. Give him the locker key.'

'But . . . ' she began. There had to be an objection to this if she could think of it. She was fearful of meeting Danny for the first time. That was it. If they were wrong, this would be a betrayal. And if they were right, how could they know how he would react? It was okay for Steven to be grinning encouragement and squeezing her hand — he wasn't going to have to do it. And Danny meant nothing to him. She found herself saying none of this and walking towards the sunshine-yellow umbrellas.

As she sat down she tried to appear natural, resisting the temptation to be glancing in all directions at once. Because how suspicious would that look? But then, surely she should appear eager to see Danny after all the interruptions. So looking round would be the natural thing to do. No, she told herself, stop this. Keep calm and concentrate on the task ahead. It was simple enough.

She looked at her watch. Steven had engineered their arrival perfectly, but without giving any impression of doing so. She had less than five minutes to wait.

This was the first time in several hours that she had been on her own. And her thoughts were running riot. Would Danny turn up at all? Steven had seemed to assume that he would, but for Danny, everything had been okay when he'd placed that letter in his mailbox. He'd had no idea about those two men who were waiting for him and what was about to happen and, since then, his life had changed. So how could they be sure Danny would come? Steven had seemed to take it for granted that he would, but how could he know? She hadn't questioned it. She wished she had.

Everything would depend on the men who were holding him. And what they wanted. But she had a horrible feeling that Steven was right about that. By the way his questioning had gone and how he'd winkled the information out of her, it seemed that he knew already.

But those men . . . If Danny had told them that she had the painting . . . No, don't go there. She only had Steven's word that this was anything to do with valuable paintings. He could have made the whole thing up. She wished they could have gone and checked her luggage as she had wanted. The doubts were swimming in now. Without Steven's honest eyes staring into hers, she was no longer sure. Without his hypnotic presence actually in front of her, the spell was broken.

The whole time her thoughts had been whirling, she had been scanning the crowds. Her heart leapt. Yes. There was Danny now, looking just the same, as if nothing had happened. She jumped up and waved; her delighted relief was so great that she was hardly aware of whether this would be a good idea or not.

Danny had seen her. He half raised a hand and nodded in recognition. Now he was beginning to move towards her, through the red tables and then the green tables belonging to the other cafés. He was looking around as he walked. Well, even as he got closer he seemed okay; there were no injuries that she could see — but he didn't seem all that happy to see her. Where was the trademark joyous devil-may-care Danny grin?

Suddenly she became aware of rapid footsteps behind her. Someone grabbed her arm and began to pull her away.

She heard Steven's voice.

'Come on, Emma. Hurry. Don't argue.'

She was obeying without thinking, not that he was giving her much opportunity to object. As they left the square, they were almost running.

'What are you doing?' she gasped. 'Danny was there. I saw him.'

'And he wasn't alone. I half thought that might happen. A risk worth taking, I thought. I was wrong.'

Emma was still trying to make sense of this as he pulled her along. Her legs were moving faster than they ever had before, taking longer strides than she would have believed possible. Cold, dry breaths were making her throat ache.

Dodging round corners, she glimpsed an old church looming ahead as they ran out into another, much larger square, side-stepping the strolling crowds. The whole place seemed so busy. People were gathered around watching something or other. There must be something on, some kind of festival, Emma thought. That was good. Crowds meant they could hide easily.

Was anyone still following? Steven didn't seem to want to stop and look. Already they were out of the vast square on the opposite side and round the side of a large building that she guessed might be a town hall. Diving inside an open doorway. At random — or did he have any idea of where they were going? She didn't care. She had to stop. She swayed against a wall, gasping. No breath left to tell him she just couldn't run any further. Emma saw that they were in a long dim corridor with doors on either side — and a woman was coming towards them. She didn't seem too happy to see them. Now she was meeting them with an irate flood of Dutch.

Steven answered meekly, seeming to be apologising for something. For bursting in on her? Oh, dear, looked like they were about to be thrown out. If anyone had chased after them this far, they might be right outside.

The woman changed to English, as so many of the Dutch seemed able to do, without thinking about it.

'Well, it's good of you to stand in, I suppose,' she said grudgingly. 'Here are the costumes. And the buckets. You are to follow alongside the procession and hand these out to the crowd.'

'What?' Emma felt as if she had stumbled into a mad dream. But Steven was gripping her arm again and she knew better than to argue. Go with the flow, she thought, why not? Might as well.

'Fortunately the costumes are one size to fit all,' the woman said. 'Here. They are to be worn over your own clothes. Return them to this room, afterwards, please.'

Emma looked at the bundle of material thrust into her arms. Red with large black spots and a black, close-fitting hood with feelers? Her eyes widened.

'Yes, it is good of you to stand in,' the

woman said again, softening a little. 'Even if you are late. The theme of the festival for this year is the insect kingdom, of course. Be glad you do not have the spider costume — that one is very unwieldy.' She turned away, doubtless hurrying off to organise something else.

'I'm sure,' Emma said faintly.

Steven had wasted no time and had quickly transformed himself into a sinister-looking beetle, all in black. He grinned at her.

'At least we are now completely unrecognisable. No need to run.'

'Just as well. I couldn't have managed any more running.' Emma's voice was muffled as she tried to arrange her feelers. 'Unrecognisable as long as the festival lasts anyway. We'll only blend in as long as we're here.' She giggled suddenly, picturing a search being set up for two human-sized creepy-crawlies. But only for a moment. Steven had some explaining to do. 'Why did you rush me off like that? Danny was there.

He was coming over to me. Did you really see the other two?'

'Yes. I suddenly realised how much danger I was putting you in. Those two were there as well — and, by sheer luck, not far from where I was. But then, I'd chosen the best place to stand, with the best view of you. And so had they.'

'So had Danny escaped from them? Were they following him to get to the painting?'

'I'm sorry.' She couldn't see Steven's face properly as it was partly obscured by black fabric but there seemed to be genuine regret in his voice. 'He was speaking to them. Before he set off towards you. It looked like some kind of plan and all three were a part of it. He didn't look as if he was being forced into anything.'

'We'll never know, will we?' Emma muttered. 'Couldn't you have waited until I'd given him the key? They would have lost interest in me, once I'd handed that over and explained. You've no chance of waiting at Rotterdam station to pick him up now.'

'It was a snap decision,' Steven admitted. 'Okay, I panicked. I couldn't bear to see you in that position. Or to run any risk of them taking you. I don't know what I was thinking about, even suggesting it.'

'I still think it might have worked,' Emma said. 'I knew there were risks. I'd agreed.' But she was looking at Steven from a new perspective. Did this mean that he cared for her a little? Might even be attracted to her? And if so, she knew that it was a two-way process. 'Well, thanks,' she continued brightly. 'Don't worry, I'm sure I can contact Danny when they're not looking. There should be plenty of opportunity dressed like this. I have to say, this stage of the plan is a master-stroke.'

Steven said nothing. He picked up his bucket.

'So what's in these buckets?' Emma persisted. 'Is this part of the plan? Are we to make contact with your police team and pass them things?'

'No plan I'm afraid. I was winging it. Open door, mistaken identity, seize the opportunity. So what have we got in here?' He took out a handful of brightly coloured folded papers.

Emma looked at hers. Purple, orange and blue with messages inside.

'They're very pretty. Are they adverts?'

'Poems. This one's something to do with flowers and sunshine and having a happy day.'

'What a lovely idea.' And something she could make use of. If she did see Danny in the crowd, this could be a way of making contact without alerting his minders. She had to believe that he was working under duress somehow. He would never have intended her to come to any harm, however badly he'd been threatened — or worse.

If she could write something on one of these papers, she could pass him a message. Her backpack was safely concealed under her red and black carapace and therefore out of reach for now — but she thought she could get to the pen in her jacket pocket.

'The procession will be entering the far side of the square very shortly,' Steven said. 'And we may as well follow the instructions because, for us, the procession is the safest place to be. Make sure you keep close to me, keep your head down, and if we spot our friends, make sure you steer well clear.'

Should she let him in on her plans or not? Even as a beetle, when he looked at her like that, she just had to believe in him all over again. But that didn't mean she was going to let him have his own way over everything without a discussion.

'But there's no chance of our being recognised now,' she said. 'This could be our last opportunity for giving Danny the key.'

He gripped her arm urgently.

'No, I thought I made it clear. That was a totally stupid idea. I'm not risking your safety, whatever the possible outcome. You're too . . . '

'Too what?'

'Never mind.'

'If you were going to chicken out like that, it's a pity you couldn't have waited a few moments more. Danny would have been preoccupied with the key and where the painting was. After I'd told him that, nobody would have been bothered about me. Now we have to start again and think of something else.'

'I told you, I acted on impulse as soon as I saw them moving towards you. But I'm even more convinced that my instincts were right. They could have taken you as a hostage — a lever to get Danny to do what they want. Even to get me off their backs. As to what to do next — don't worry about that. This isn't your problem.'

'Not my problem?' Emma hissed crossly. 'My boyfriend is in the power of a gang of criminals, I may have an undiscovered and stolen Vermeer in my luggage and I'm skulking around Delft dressed as a ladybird with no idea what's going to happen next — and you say it's not my problem? Oh, well, fine.

I won't worry then. Great.'

'I meant I don't want you to be involved anymore. Not if we can avoid it. I'll handle everything from here on in. Look, stick close to me in the thick of the crowd. Maybe when the procession ends or the entertainment is concluding and all the other insects are metamorphosing. That will be the best time to ditch our costumes and make our escape. No one will notice us.'

'But — '

'Can't talk anymore now — here's the procession. OK?'

It didn't seem to make any difference whether she agreed with this plan or not, Emma thought. If you could call it a plan. Lucky she hadn't told him her idea for arranging another meeting with Danny. No way would Steven have let that happen. It was good that he felt protective and that was enjoyable in a way — but enough was enough. Now his concern was proving an obstacle. And her idea seemed so obvious. The only way forward. Well, when she saw

Danny, she would sort it out for herself. A pity she couldn't just pass him the luggage locker key but now that was out of reach in her backpack. A pity she hadn't thought of that as she struggled into the costume, but things had been happening so quickly and she'd had no time to think.

They were joining the procession now and blending in. A walking procession of giant and fantastical insect creatures, wobbling their ungainly way through the crowds in the square and out through the narrow cobbled streets.

Emma walked along with her yellow bucket, smiling and handing out the brightly coloured pieces of paper. But all the time she was planning her next move.

What should she write on a note to Danny? She would have to keep to time and place she supposed. And that was only the start. She would have to get away from Steven somehow to keep the appointment. Or he would be there, right by her side, protecting her yet again.

And there was no guarantee that she would spot Danny in the crowd. Although presumably he and his minders would still be looking for her. Searching for a girl with shoulder length blonde hair, in jeans and a sage green jacket.

Their chances of finding her in this throng would be slim anyway. She frowned. Well, first, get the note written so at least she would be ready if the chance came.

Steven was looking away from her, scanning the crowd as she was but for very different motives. She felt guilty for deceiving him. Yes, she had to admit she was attracted to him, but she still couldn't get round a sense of niggling doubt. Even if he was with the police, some of his ideas didn't seem to make complete sense. How did she know she could really trust him? And if Danny needed her help to get out of this, she couldn't just ditch him.

She wished she knew more about the men who had kidnapped him and whether the left luggage key was going to be enough to placate them. Hopefully, Danny would pass the key to them and they would collect the painting and be picked up instead of him. Best all round.

Steven was swept up for an impromptu dance with a green caterpillar. Yes, now, while he was distracted — and before the caterpillar moved on to her. She wriggled a little, found the pen and opened a red note. She scrawled inside: *Meet me in half an hour by the Old Church*. That would be a good place. No mistaking the large church in the great square. She refolded the note and slipped it safely inside her black glove. Now, she was ready.

She fixed a smile on her face and set off again. The crowds were lining the street on both sides now; she tried to choose the side away from Steven but, of course, that didn't work. He was slipping across in between the giant hoverflies in a flash, keeping first a couple of steps in front of her and then moving behind her. She didn't like that. Him being so close made it more difficult to hide her movements. The caterpillar had been a real stroke of luck but now it had moved on. Perhaps she could concentrate on engaging with the crowd. That would give her the chance to get behind him again.

Emma discovered quickly that if she spoke first, in English, the Dutch would automatically answer in the same language. No need then to have to admit she couldn't understand them. 'Have a small poem,' she said, 'for a happy day. Your very own poem.' The people she spoke to smiled and laughed and she smiled back. She was even beginning to enjoy herself.

She turned to see how Steven was getting on and was surprised to see no sign of him. How odd — all that insistence on how she must stick by him and now he was the one to go wandering off. With a vague ripple of unease, she wondered if he was all right.

A gap formed swiftly among the cheerful faces and at the back of the street, near the shops, she saw Steven, deep in conversation with someone. There could be no mistake. It was one of the men in the dark coats. The ones in the car and who had gone up to the apartment.

The crowd jostled back and hid her view. Her heart was thudding. No. It was the same man. She bit her lips together, not sure what to do. And here was a face she knew very well indeed, standing right in front of her. Two eyes peering into hers.

'Emma?'

'Danny!' Taken by surprise, she couldn't think straight. 'Are you ok?'

'I can't talk now,' he replied.

'I understand.' Without thinking about it, she passed him her note.

He took it, read it and nodded before grinning briefly.

'Okay. And thanks for the rainbow.'

'What?' Whatever was he talking about? Suddenly, she realised. Of course, he had read the poem. She hadn't had a clue what that red piece of paper had wished. And she hadn't known Danny's Dutch was that good. But if he were deeply involved in some criminal ring, as Steven had told her, she supposed it would have to be. If she could believe anything Steven told her. Her heart contracted painfully. She no longer knew which side anyone was on.

Danny was already sliding away.

'Will you be able to get away — from them?' she said desperately, hardly wanting to let him go.

The old grin.

'I'll get away from my minders if you get away from yours.'

And perhaps, after what she had just seen, they were one and the same. And that meant it was Emma and Danny against everyone else.

'Yes, I'll do that,' she said, and swiftly he was gone and she was left passing poems to a family group of two children in long shorts and a man in red trousers.

5

So she'd done it. She had made the arrangement with Danny and now she was thinking furiously about how she would keep to it. And Steven had betrayed her. Hadn't he? She frowned, thinking furiously but still not wanting to believe in what she had seen. Perhaps there could be some explanation. Perhaps he'd acted on impulse again, to gain information somehow, and would tell her all about it when he saw her. Perhaps he had been offering the man a poem, while maintaining his disguise. She hoped so. Some illogical feminine instinct wanted to believe that he was still on her side. But avoid Steven for now, she told herself, go it alone for the meeting with Danny and she would be keeping her options open.

Half an hour. As soon as she left the protection of the procession, she must dump her costume somewhere. Otherwise she would stick out like a sore thumb. Besides, Danny knew about her disguise now. She would just have to hope that his captors didn't make him pass on the information.

Another thought occurred to her. Wait a minute — they hadn't been acting like captors. Maybe at the Beastmarket they had been keeping their eyes on him as well as her, but here, they hadn't been close to Danny at all. He could have run off any time. So why hadn't he? Perhaps it wasn't that simple. Perhaps he had been instructed to find her and they were keeping a close watch on him. Maybe they were watching her even now, waiting. They might have weapons. There might be more than two of them. She shivered. Thinking like this wasn't helpful.

The procession was moving slowly but surely, further away from the main square and the old church — but she could still get back there fairly quickly, five or ten minutes at most. Over a canal they went, along a shady pavement, through an archway.

Yet another area of old buildings, this time around a small courtyard with an alleyway leading out and another canal beyond. Journey's end it seemed; the medley of strange creatures was disappearing through a large open door into a building on the left. Time to leave. There could be some kind of roll call coming up or at least a social event. That meant that people might start asking who she was.

Emma hung back, still distributing poems as she looked round for any of the others. The crowd was gathering for what seemed to be a final performance involving balloons, flutes and trumpets and a gathering of millipedes. Emma glanced round quickly and nipped through a gate on her right. Not a moment too soon because there was the large black beetle. Had he seen her? She didn't think so. He was hurrying on into the building ahead. Looking for her probably.

She glanced round quickly. She was now in a small garden belonging to what seemed to be a museum — attached to yet another church. Easy to dodge behind a couple of flowering shrubs and deposit the costume and the bucket. Hopefully the museum curator would eventually find it and return it to the town hall. No time to worry too much about that unfortunately.

Steven hadn't come out again. Yes, there was another performance going on in there. Through the open doors she could hear cheering and applause. And the way the mixed crowd of people and insects were all crammed together inside, it would take Steven some time to realise that she wasn't in there.

No one else paid any attention to her as she retraced her steps — and why should they? All the same, she felt vulnerable now. Perhaps she should have stuck with the procession to the bitter end. After that, she could have borrowed a discarded costume from someone else and emerged as an anonymous greenfly or bluebottle.

She wouldn't have been too obvious; people would just assume that she was making her way home in costume for some reason. A pity she hadn't thought of that sooner. Too late now. She had come too far in those few minutes to go back. But there could be another way round it. She remembered how Steven had turned his jacket inside out . . .

She was back in the large square now, which was lined with souvenir shops — the distinctive blue and white Delft pottery being a favourite buy — but there were racks of cheap clothes, too. Feeling a slight pang as she remembered Steven's advice, she chose a bright orange t-shirt and a red baseball cap. You certainly couldn't miss these colours.

She smiled her relief at the shop assistant and bit her tongue. That had been close. She had only just stopped herself from saying, 'No need for a bag, I'll wear them now.' What a give-away that would have been. *I'm no good at this*, she thought. She mustn't give the bored-looking girl any reason to remember her. You never knew. She must concentrate on being as normal as possible. Blend in.

Behind the postcard racks and checking that no one was watching, Emma pulled the new t-shirt over her original one, and pushed her hair under the cap. A small detour to add a new pair of sunglasses from the adjoining shop and at once she felt better. And, of course, she did need the carrier bag for her green jacket. No one glancing swiftly into the crowds would recognise her now.

If only she knew who to trust. She liked Steven, but the more she considered the way he was acting, the more he worried her. Okay, he must surely be able to explain everything when he could find the time — or would he? Their first plan at the Beastmarket had seemed a good one to her, so why had he spoiled it? Yes, she had taken his explanation on board, but surely that was an odd way for a policeman to behave? And what about his excuse for not involving the Rotterdam police? She wasn't sure that made too much sense.

At least she knew he was a policeman. She had seen his identity card herself and even before he had told her what he did. That was proof. She frowned, rearranging the sunglasses on her nose with one finger, recalling how he had thrown his jacket carelessly on the chair in front of her.

A bit risky, leaving his ID lying about like that. Almost as if he wanted her to find it. A cold shiver ran all the way down her back. Anyone could fake an ID. She couldn't remember ever seeing a genuine police ID. She just wouldn't have known whether Steven's card was a genuine form of police identification or not.

Emma felt bereft. Standing in the crowds milling around outside the old church, she had never felt so alone. At least Steven had seemed to be on her side and had always seemed to know what to do. And she had trusted his authority. Now, she was almost a hundred per cent certain that he had deceived her. She was on her own.

She straightened her shoulders. No, not entirely alone. She couldn't believe or disbelieve or dismiss any of it on the small pieces of evidence she had. First she must listen to what Danny had to say.

She looked at her watch, feeling uneasy. Where was Danny? Surely he would turn up? He wanted the painting too much. Or his package, at least. She only had Steven's word for it that the package was a valuable painting.

In Delft, she realised now, Vermeer had a very high profile. There was even a Vermeer trail, marked with large cube-shaped information stands. There was one not a few feet from where she was standing. She edged over and began reading it. She would look less conspicuous that way. It was interesting, too. A pity she couldn't concentrate properly.

A guided tour had paused next to her, blocking her view and she joined the fringes of the group. This would enable her to see Danny before he saw her, to make sure he was on his own. Particularly as he was now late.

The guide was speaking in English, reciting what had been on the information cube almost word for word. Hardly surprising she supposed. They must repeat this several times a day.

'And behind where I stand, in the New Church is where the Vermeer family would have worshipped and where the artist's wife and parents are buried. Vermeer himself, however, is buried in the Old Church — we will come to that later . . . '

Emma stared at him, oblivious of everyone around her. Old Church? She had assumed that this was the Old Church — and that was what she had written in her note. How old did a church have to be to be called old, for goodness sake? But this was her own fault, she should have checked. Ridiculous. A historic town like Delft would have dozens of churches. She should have been clearer. She hadn't had time to think it out properly. She hurried through the group and tapped the guide on the arm.

'Excuse me, where is the Old Church?'

He didn't seem too happy at the interruption.

'As I said, if you will just be patient, we shall come to that in a few moments.'

'No — please. It's very important.'

'You are interrupting my tour.'

'If you'll just tell me, I'll get out of your way. I promise.'

'Oh, very well.' He gestured angrily, back towards the town hall. 'Out of the Great Market and turn right, over the canal. You will see it through the archway.'

'Thank you so much.' Emma felt like kissing him. Or perhaps not. How could she have been so stupid? And now, darting through the crowds like an arrow and calling apologies, she was attracting all the attention she didn't want. But she had to get there before Danny gave up. She was late already. How long would he wait?

There was a dense crowd blocking her way now — applauding an act taking place on the street. She tried to dodge amongst them — and a hand grabbed her arm, pulling her into a narrow alleyway between two buildings.

'What are you playing at, babe?' Danny hissed. 'Taking me for a fool, were you, having me hanging around in the wrong place?'

'No!' She was gasping for breath. 'Made a mistake. Wrong church.'

'Your idea.'

'I know. Sorry.'

'I haven't much time. Where's that parcel I gave you?'

Emma glared at him. How about how happy he was to see her and an apology or two?

'I need to know what it is and how you got it. Because a lot of odd things have happened to me since I was supposed to meet you at the flat. Disturbing things. I need to know what this is all about.'

He hesitated.

'Better for you if you don't know.'

'I'll be the judge of that. How much better for me than seeing you being dragged into a car and those men setting off up to the flat? And where are they now? How are you walking around without them? Have they let you go? And why?'

'Because I told them what they wanted to hear. That I could collect it myself, from you, and I'd do a better job on my own.'

'Okay.' That made sense, she supposed. 'What will they do to you if you don't get it?'

'I don't intend to find out.' He leaned against the wall, blocking her way out of the alley. Only yards away, there were people chattering and laughing out in the sunshine and yet here in the shadows, she and Danny seemed cut off from the rest of the world. 'And I don't need to find out. Because you're going to give it back to me.'

'And you're going to tell me what this is about,' Emma repeated. 'You don't frighten me, Danny.' Her heart was thudding. If she held her breath, perhaps he wouldn't hear it. She stared at him without blinking.

He was the first to look away, with a forced laugh.

'What are we doing? We're on the same side, you and me.'

Are we? Emma thought. I don't know which side anyone's on. I don't even know what the sides are. She stared up at him. Giving Danny the key to the locker would be so easy. It would all be finished with. She could go straight home and leave them all to get on with it. But whatever he had done, Danny had meant a lot to her not so very long ago. If Steven had been telling her the truth, as soon as Danny pulled her bag from the locker, he could be arrested. Perhaps he deserved to be. But she wanted and indeed needed to be sure.

His face was very close to hers.

'Come on, babe. You know I love you.' She closed her eyes as he kissed her. She tried to kiss him back, wanting to recapture the emotion but the turmoil in her head was getting in the way of that weak-at-the-knees feeling. If she was still capable of feeling it. She had almost forgotten the original purpose of her visit.

She broke away first, feeling sorry for him. He had no idea he was undergoing her own private trial as well as everything else. Whatever happened, she felt that Danny just couldn't win.

'It would help if you could be straight with me,' she said, perhaps too gently. 'What's in the package?'

His face was dark.

'Do you need to ask? You know already. Don't tell me you didn't look at it — as soon as you got on the ferry in Hull. Before the boat even left. Anyone would have done.'

Emma looked at him sadly.

'No, they wouldn't. I didn't.'

'More fool you. But you know now, don't you? Your new friend has made certain of that, hasn't he?'

'Yes. He's told me what he suspects.' She could have tried to deny it but what was the point? There had been too many denials and concealing of truths already. 'I think it's a previously unknown painting. By Vermeer.' Danny gave a sharp intake of breath. Perhaps he had been calling her bluff and got more than he bargained for. 'It's time for the truth, Danny. I need to know. Where did you get it? And what are you going to do with it?'

'Oh, it's definitely mine,' he said quickly. 'No problem there. A client gave it to me. I'd been helping her with her investments — she gave it to me instead of a fee. Asked if I minded!' He grinned. 'She was more than happy when I said I didn't. So everyone was happy. Okay?'

'Did she know it was a Vermeer?'

He shrugged.

'Didn't ask. Let's face it, I didn't

know myself. I took a risk. Could have lost out after all that work. Just had a feeling about it.'

Emma gasped. The painting would be worth far, far more than any fee Danny could earn. She could imagine the client, an unsuspecting old lady perhaps, falling for Danny's charm. Emma determined that when this was over, she would find out who the mystery client was and make sure that they at least received a fair share. That should be possible, surely? But for now, there were more urgent things to consider. Like how to get herself out of all this.

'If it's all above board, then why did I have to bring it over secretly? Why didn't *you* bring it? And where do those horrible men come into it?'

The old Danny swagger was apparent once more.

'I want the best deal, don't I? They represent a private collector. Someone who will pay well over the odds to ensure this painting stays out of the public eye. And if he's that rich, he's entitled to a mad idea or two if you ask me. Why should I care?' There was that smile again, the old beguiling smile that had captivated her from the start. 'It's the whole truth, Emma. It's legally mine and I have every right to sell it. So where is it?'

His answers all seemed genuine. She had engineered this meeting to hear his side of the story and now she had. And yet she was still hesitating. He had called her Emma. He very rarely did that. Such a small thing and yet her instincts were screaming at her. He was holding something back.

'It's in my bag,' she said carefully. 'In a left luggage locker. At the station.'

He exhaled a long breath of satisfaction.

'Right.' He paused. It was a long pause for Danny, but there was a lot to think about.

'Do we just give the key to those men who are representing your buyer?' she asked. 'Or what?'

‘Not sure that would be too great an idea. No room for manoeuvre then, have I? No, that would be a move too soon. I’m not going there until someone pays me.’

‘I suppose not.’ For one joyful moment, she’d thought that would be the answer to everything. No one would be too worried if the messenger boys in black were picked up by the police. Their employer would get them out of any trouble by merely picking up a phone. And why should she worry if Danny was intercepted? He would only need to prove his ownership, which might take a while but would lead her to the elderly client and ensure that Emma could see she was fairly treated. A big advantage there. Her betrayal would mean the end of her relationship with Danny, but that had been on the cards anyway. She removed the baseball cap and shook her hair back from her face. Perhaps that was part of the problem. Perhaps there was no elderly client and Danny could not prove it was his . . .

'Okay, let's go,' Danny said suddenly.

'What are we going to do? Do you want the key?'

'Not yet, babe. Let's see how the land lies when we get there, shall we? You see, I just have this funny feeling that there's something you're not telling me.' She had no chance to try to deny it because he was pulling her along, not back towards the Great Market, but deeper into the winding alleys. 'Here we go.' Two bikes were leaning against a wall in the passageway. Before Emma could protest, Danny had darted through an open doorway and returned pulling a hooded top over his head. 'Someone's washing but almost dry — lucky thing that. That'll disguise me nicely.' He seized the handlebars of the larger bike. 'That one's yours.'

'Danny! What do you think you're doing? We can't just take these.'

'Oh, when I'm in the money I'll bring them a wad of compensation or something,' he said airily.

'Haven't you any money to pay now?'

‘No time.’

‘Yes, we have.’ Emma scrabbled in her backpack. ‘I’ve got enough to pay for the top at least.’ She tried her pockets and found one of the happy day poems. *Sorry, urgent need.* She scrawled. *One top, two bikes. Thanks.* She bent to leave the money and the note sticking out from under a stone.

Danny laughed.

‘Trust you, sweetheart. Don’t worry about the bikes. Everyone knows bikes in Holland are free to all. Community transport.’

Reluctantly she gripped her handlebars.

‘Are we cycling back to Rotterdam?’

‘What planet are you on?’ His laughter was unkind. ‘No, we’ll go to the station here, in Delft. That way, we’ll end up directly where we need to be. So if you’ve finished throwing your money around, let’s go.’

Yes. The sooner this was over and done with, the better. Emma glanced round, trying to make sure that no one was following them as they swerved and swayed along through the narrow streets.

There was no sign of anyone with short haircuts and black coats. She jerked her head back as a car hooted at her. And no sign of any giant beetles. Or that distinctive orange jacket. She sighed. As far as Steven was concerned, she wasn't sure whether to be glad or sorry.

6

As they ditched their bikes and caught the train, Emma began to relax a little. There was no sign of any pursuit. So far, so good. Danny put his arm around her and started telling her about how well some deal was going. Something to do with a small firm selling bolts.

Emma tried to pay attention, but surely there were more important things he could be talking about? Perhaps he wanted to look and sound completely normal but no one on the train seemed at all interested in them. They were surrounded by ordinary couples and families going back to the city after a fun day out. Whenever Emma tried to raise the subject of what Danny would do when he had the painting and how he was going to meet up with the would-be customers, the men in black coats, he started off on something else.

She felt a twinge of annoyance. He had always had a habit of skittering off onto his own concerns whenever you tried to pin him down. Ignoring whatever she was trying to say. How could she not have realised just how irritating he could be? Okay, don't tell me then, she muttered to herself. Do what you like. Just as long as you leave me out of it.

Danny leapt up even before the train began to slow down, taking her by surprise. Emma's heart was thumping now. This was it. Central Station, Rotterdam. Easily recognisable, even though she was now arriving from a different direction.

So much had happened since she had arrived there that morning she could hardly believe that it still looked exactly the same. If anyone should be watching out for them, it would be here. She felt almost certain that Steven would have set something up. No wonder he hadn't bothered to chase after the bikes or the train. He knew they would turn up here.

Danny hung back as they came into the entrance hall.

'Okay, you go and get it.'

'Me?' Emma's voice was a squeak. That wasn't what she'd intended.

'Sure. It's your locker. I'll wait over there. By the way out.'

She gave him a quick look. Was he just being cautious or did he suspect something? She should have thought of that and been ready with an excuse. Too late now as Danny was already moving away.

She felt in her pocket for the key, her hands trembling. Now she was having a blank and worrying moment of not being able to remember which locker was hers. Hardly surprising. It seemed a lifetime ago when she had happily locked her bag away, pleased to be rid of the weight. She tried to resist the urge to look over her shoulder, which would only make her look suspicious. And if anyone should be observing her, what was she going to do about it?

She felt surprised recognition when the locker door opened and her bag was there, waiting like an old familiar friend. The one dependable item in this mad new existence she was suddenly experiencing. She felt a ridiculous urge to give it a hug. But, of course, she didn't. How stupid would that be? She pulled it out and set off across the open space of the entrance, looking down at the mottled grey flooring.

At any moment she might feel a hand on her shoulder. Or Steven's voice accusing her of running out on him. And she would have no defence to make. There would be very little humour in his voice now. He would be fuming. He had been reluctant to trust her in the first place; how would he feel about her after this?

Perhaps she had been wrong to go with the wild impulse that had caused the disguised ladybird to take off without an escort. Perhaps Steven had merely been handing the man in the suit a happy-day poem. But also she had needed to give Danny the chance to speak up for himself. And now that she had, was she any the wiser?

The fifteen minute train journey had been a wasted opportunity, leaving her with the few garbled excuses he had come out with in Delft. She had made her choice, however, and must make the best of it.

'Don't look round,' Danny said abruptly from close behind her shoulder. 'Keep going.' She could hear the tension in his voice as he fell into step beside her.

'Where to?'

'It's okay. Just walk with me. We'll go and see what we've got.'

'I'm sure it is okay, Danny. But can you just stop telling me that it is?' She tried to make a joke of the remark but she knew that her laughter sounded false.

They crossed a busy main road, retracing the steps she had taken that morning. There was the turning where she had struck off to the shopping precinct but this time they kept straight on, keeping to the main road until Danny entered a bar on a corner. This was where the Coolsingel street took off, she realised.

Much further down, she glimpsed the red brick tower that was Danny's apartment building before Danny was gesturing to her impatiently and she too was inside the bar. Dark wood and an old-fashioned feel with lots of shadowy corners. Emma could see why Danny had chosen to come here. He led her to a table in one of the booths, protected by carved screens, but with a view of another entrance leading to a small side street.

Emma set her bag on the seat between them, so it was hidden by the table. Danny was hardly looking at her. His eyes were roving around the other customers from one entrance to the other.

'Ok. Give, babe.'

An offer of a drink would be good, Emma thought. Obviously that wasn't going to happen.

'I'm afraid I put it right at the bottom. To keep it flat.' She unzipped the bag and began rooting through make-up and spare underwear, aware that beside her Danny was hardly able to keep his hands from twitching. At any minute, he would be diving in himself. Which wouldn't help. 'Here it is. It's all right, Danny. I hadn't lost it.' That was meant as a joke, but Danny wasn't taking it that way. He was almost snatching the package from her. He dithered for a moment or two, obviously undecided whether to open it with care or tear the wrappings off. 'Do you want to borrow my nail scissors?' she asked.

'What? Oh — yes. Ta.'

* * *

Emma stared as the paper fell away, Danny scrabbled impatiently through several sheets of A4 paper and the painting was revealed.

'Wow,' she said. 'It's lovely.' The colours were as bright as if it had been painted yesterday. She tilted her head as if that would help her to see it better, thinking. She didn't know why, but something didn't seem quite right. The words of a TV art expert came back to her out of the blue: trust your instincts. And her instincts were shrieking — but she wasn't sure why.

The work was competent and the subject matter spot-on. From the few details she had gleaned from the Vermeer trail in Delft and Danny's Internet research, she knew that Vermeer had favoured seventeenth century domestic interiors. And here was a woman standing at a table, kneading a lump of dough. Hence Danny's joke in his note, she supposed. A servant maybe, though she seemed neatly dressed in a gown of dull yellow and a white apron, her hair concealed under an unflattering cap.

'What do you think?'

'It's lovely. But are you sure it's a

genuine Vermeer?' She was hesitant, thinking he might be angry, but he didn't seem to be.

'What's the matter with it?'

'I don't know. I can't quite put my finger on it.'

'But you know about paintings.'

'What? Not really. Oh, I did my General Studies essay on the History of Art, is that what you mean? But I didn't touch on Vermeer.'

'And what about your ex?'

She did a double take.

'My ex? Oh, you mean, Mike? The antiques dealer? I haven't heard from him in ages. Did I tell you about him? I'd forgotten. My goodness, he was charming and polite and attentive, but he was just so boring. That sounds dreadful, I felt really guilty when I broke it off. But he would only talk about what he was doing and his interests, you know?' Exactly as Danny tended to do. Mmm. Of course, the 'trust your instincts' quote came from him. How could she have ever forgotten? She had had art and antiques coming out of her ears.

'You must have absorbed some of what he told you.'

'Yes, I expect I did.' She looked at the painting again, half closing her eyes. 'I'm no expert. But if an expert told me it was genuine, I would have to go along with that. Yes, I'm sure it's okay.' She sat back, nodding firmly.

Danny lounged back in his seat, grinning.

'There's something I have to tell you. It isn't.'

'What?' Emma was shocked. Her voice came out as a squeak. 'But what about those men? And selling it to the private collector? How will he react if it's a fake?'

'I thought it was genuine at first,' Danny said. 'That's why I made the arrangements to sell it. Now I think it's a very good attempt by a pupil. Someone living at the same time as Vermeer. Or just after.'

'Did Vermeer have any pupils?'

Danny shrugged.

'He must have done. Didn't all painters have pupils in those days?'

So did this mean that Danny hadn't deceived his elderly customer when he took the painting? Not necessarily. A pupil's work could still be worth a substantial amount.

'But you've told your private collector about this?' she asked, but the smug grin on his face gave her the answer. 'No, you haven't. But, Danny, you already know what he's capable of. Isn't this very dangerous? What will happen when he finds out?'

'I intend to be well away by then. I mean, we will. You and I. It won't really matter.'

If she'd had any last doubts, Danny had just quashed them. It certainly would not matter to Emma because she would be having no part at all in Danny's future. Her decision was made.

'You worry too much,' he said carelessly. 'It'll all work out. And now I need to contact our friends again — but on my terms this time. And I'm not taking the painting with me.' He took out his mobile phone. 'Hold the painting up, Emma. Smile, please.'

Bemused, Emma found herself doing as he asked before working it out.

'Oh, you want to prove to them that you've found me and that I have it.'

'Got it in one. This will be enough to get them to advance me some of the money I've asked for. With any luck, they'll give me the rest when I hand it over. But, if not, I'll settle for that. That's the plan. That way, they won't be expecting me to do a runner. I could even suggest, if they seem doubtful, that they take it to their boss for his verification and I'll meet up with them tomorrow or whenever to get the rest. I shan't, obviously, if they're that mistrustful. But we'll see how it goes.'

'And what am I going to be doing? Do I wait here?'

'No way. Too risky.'

'Not back at the flat?' She shivered. She really didn't want to return there.

He shook his head.

'I have more than one address. Comes in handy for all kinds of things.'

Yes, Emma could see that. Somewhere inconspicuous, tucked away down a side street. She could just picture it.

'I'll give you the address and directions. And a key, of course. Mustn't forget that. And from the window, you'll be able to look over the café in the old harbour where I intend to meet them. You can watch the developments.'

'And if the meeting doesn't go well? If it doesn't work out as you're hoping? What then?' This all sounded very dubious to her.

'Don't worry, babe. It'll be — '

'Okay. Yes, I know. But if it isn't?'

'Tell you what, we'll have a signal. If I put both hands up in the air — like this — it means 'Run.' Go. Take the painting and get out of there.'

'Won't they think that's odd?' She frowned incredulously.

'If it gets to that, things will be so bad that it won't matter what they think. Trust me, babe.' He leaned forward and unexpectedly kissed her.

In spite of all her resolves, Emma found herself kissing him back — but her adrenalin was racing because of the danger. This had to be part of her goodbye to him, she told herself. But she could hardly tell him that now, with all this going on.

'We'll be ok leaving here together,' he said abruptly. 'On second thoughts, might as well show you myself. Don't want you to get lost, do we?'

'I don't think that's too likely. Since I found your other flat on my own — '

He was no longer listening.

'Come on.'

She leapt up and raced after him. Not more rushing about. She would be incredibly fit after all this. He stopped suddenly as if he'd just thought of something and she cannoned into him, her bag banging her hip painfully.

'Ow, Danny!'

'Tell you what, leave all that bulky packaging in the flat when you go. Not easy to carry. That was only to get you through customs or whatever. There are some folders in the top drawer of my desk. Put you-know-what in one of those.'

'That hurt, Danny.'

'What?'

'When you stopped.'

'Oh. Right. Sorry.' He looked down at her bag. 'Shall I carry that?' It was the first time he'd offered. But that was Danny. You accepted him as he was, or you got left behind. And after this week, she would make sure that she was left well behind. She didn't want to go in the same direction. She could hardly believe that she had thought Danny and his way of life to be exciting and fun. How could she have been so stupid? She passed the bag over to him.

'Good grief! What have you got in here? No, don't answer that.' He was off and she was almost breaking into a trot to catch up. Fortunately they were setting off along Coolsingel yet again with its wide pavements; she didn't hold out much hope for anyone who got in Danny's way.

She wondered whether passing directly below Danny's flat was a good idea. Could there still be someone watching it? But before they reached it, Danny was striking off to the left, past the old town hall and then the old Laurenskirk, behind the town hall and away from the main streets. Here the surroundings were quieter and scruffier with graffiti in evidence again, but there was nothing to cause concern, and shortly they were leaving the graffiti behind and emerging into a vast paved open space. Bright and clean and modern. In the centre was a glass and metal structure which Emma thought at first must be another of the abstract sculptures that were dotted around the city.

Danny set off across the white paving slabs without hesitation, but Emma felt very conspicuous. If anyone should be trying to follow, she and Danny would be an obvious quarry here. As they neared the glass structure, she realised that it wasn't a sculpture, but the entrance to an underground station. She hurried after him with her head down. Perhaps they would look as if they were hurrying to catch a train. But no, because they had passed the way in and the downwards escalator without pausing.

Where could they be going? She risked a glance ahead and did a double take. An inconspicuous side street? No way. She should have realised — that wasn't Danny's style. She recognised the buildings they were approaching; she had seen them in the postcards. An interconnected set of cubes in yellow and grey, set on end, reminding her of a fairground fun house.

'You don't have an apartment here? Isn't it very expensive?'

He shrugged.

'Necessary. Impresses the clients.'

'You're not kidding.'

They were entering a small courtyard, where above them the cubes leaned inwards at various angles. How on earth could anyone live or work inside those, Emma wondered? Near to, they reminded her even more of crazy cottages at a seaside fairground. She glimpsed a direction sign indicating that one was open to the public. Yes, she could understand that.

Danny was leading the way up a narrow winding stone stairway and unlocking a door. They were inside a surprisingly normal apartment, flooded with light from windows on at least three sides, reflecting off pale wooden flooring. It had been very cleverly designed. The rooms were all angular and the large windows were set into oddly-shaped apertures, but the whole feel was of light and space.

'It's great, Danny.'

Not like Danny to pass up on praise, but he ignored the compliment.

'You can see the café from this

window, see? They're there now.'

Emma glanced down at the tables of the waterside café and, yes, there were the black coated figures that had grown so familiar to her. She didn't feel too happy about them, even if they were supposed to be working together with Danny.

'Why were they bundling you into their car?' she asked suddenly.

'What? Oh, that's the way they like to work. They want to intimidate people.' He grinned. 'They think it will stop anyone trying to fiddle them. And I pretended to be scared stiff, naturally. Okay, gotta go. Oh, you need a folder.' He pulled open a desk drawer.

'It's fine. I'll find one. You go.'

'Right. Leave the packaging on the desk.' He kissed the top of her head. 'See you. Wish me luck.' And he was gone.

Emma sighed. There were so many things she had wanted to ask and, once again, he hadn't allowed her the time. Purposely, she suspected. And why keep on and on about the padded bag? It would be good to sit down and relax for a few minutes. She felt safe here; the flat was a refuge where she could see out without being seen. But there wasn't time for that, either. She found an empty folder without any trouble and weighed it in her hand. It didn't seem all that substantial to her. Not when you considered what you would be entrusting to the flimsy cardboard. Even if the painting was a fake. Her fingers twitched. Yes, it was time for a better look. That bar had been too dark for her to see properly.

The light here was bright and unforgiving. She took the small painting in both hands and held it towards the window. No, she had been right. The subject was okay but it was obvious now that the brushstrokes were those of an amateur. How could anyone seriously think this could be a genuine Vermeer? She wasn't even convinced it was seventeenth century.

This was ridiculous. She hoped she

wasn't around when the black-coat brigade realised what they'd been wasting their time over. This wouldn't fool anyone. Okay, she would put it in a folder if that was what Danny wanted her to do. But she was strongly tempted to let that be the end of what she was doing for him. She had her bag back. She could leave now. She could get well away from here and go straight home.

The idea was tempting. She would let Danny know what she had done, of course. Once she was far away, boarding the ferry or something. That would be quite soon enough to phone or text him. But she would be dumping him as well and she had always hated the idea of doing that by phone. Unfortunately with all these complications about the painting, there didn't seem to be much alternative. And Danny, she knew, wasn't too bothered about her. Only about his clever idea, as he saw it, of getting a large sum of money for a fake.

She looked down at the café from the

window, already sending Danny a goodbye message in her mind. There he was, sitting down beside them already. They looked harmless enough from here. Two businessmen chatting over coffee. But she knew what they were capable of. Her hands reached reluctantly for her phone. Perhaps she should tell Danny she was leaving the fake painting in the flat. She had loved him once. She couldn't just dump him into a load of trouble. Those men were dangerous.

Think this through, Emma. If she left the painting here, Danny would bring the men here to collect it, for the supposed verification, and would immediately be in one big heap of trouble. They were bound to see through it. Perhaps she could take the painting straight down to them, now. She could confront them and apologise for the terrible mistake. Danny would be furious but at least he would be safe. Or would he? Who knew how they would react? He had made fools of them and they might easily become very nasty indeed. Somehow she didn't feel that those men would be too impressed by apologies.

Best for Emma to take it and put it somewhere else — back in the left luggage maybe, or at the nearest police station if she could find one. She could text Danny telling him to make himself scarce while he had the chance. Without the money if he had any sense. Although when had Danny ever had much sense? But it was the best she could think of. At any minute they would be standing up, ready to come up here. But for now they were still talking intently, perhaps arguing about the amount.

She picked up the folder and at once hit a snag. It wouldn't fit into her bag — not unless she unpacked everything. It might be lighter and flatter than the padded bag but it was larger. Trust Danny not to think of that. Emma shook her head crossly. Why make so much fuss over this bag? She looked round for something else but there wasn't anything. And there wasn't time. There was only the padded bag. And it was heavy, even being empty. She didn't know why Danny had chosen it; you could get much lighter ones. All that parcel tape, too — no wonder they had needed her scissors. You didn't need that much. Now it was sticking to her fingers and she was forgetting to watch the drama below.

Yes, he was showing them the picture on his phone. And gesturing up towards this window. She dodged back uneasily as the faces turned towards her. Was that a good idea? Danny hadn't mentioned letting them know where she was. But now they were looking away again. Time to go. This could be her only chance. But she shouldn't have messed around with the parcel tape; the whole bag was stuck to her now. Come on, she muttered. I haven't time for this. She ripped it off in a moment of panic — and the packaging came apart. Instinctively she stepped even further away from the window although there was no way they could see inside, not up here. She was staring at the torn bag in her hand.

There was something else. She should have realised. The bag felt too stiff. Cardboard, she thought, an added safeguard to keep the painting flat? But why bother when it was in a frame already? And the cardboard wasn't the plain brown surface she would have expected. She could see a hand covered in flour, a yellow sleeve rolled back, part of a table . . .

Whatever Danny was telling those men, he had intended to deceive her, too. The real Vermeer was here, in her shaking hands.

7

No wonder Danny had wanted her to leave the packaging in the flat — he had set her up. If she had to run, he wanted her to take the fake in the folder, leaving the real one here, disguised as discarded packaging. Maybe he had always intended that she should take off without him. But why?

Unfortunately it didn't take much thought to come up with a reason. She was to be a decoy, leading the men away from the flat while Danny made off with the real thing. Emma was shaking with anger. How could he do that? Any last shred of the old loyalties to Danny vanished in a white heat of rage and grief. He had betrayed her. Had she ever meant anything to him? Well, she wasn't going to sit around waiting for Danny's plan to happen. She was going now. She had wasted enough time already. And she was taking the painting — the real one. And to the nearest police station. Which she should have done in the first place. Where was that map she'd got from Tourist Information? No, never mind that — get out of here first, work out where to go later.

Emma pushed the padded bag with the real Vermeer into her backpack and glanced out of the window, as she had been doing every minute or so. She gasped in horror. Too late. Danny was already making his ridiculous arms-in-the-air signal. As, of course, he had planned to do all along. That meant he wanted her to run. She would have to leave her large bag here. She couldn't escape pursuit staggering along with that. Perhaps they would waste a few vital minutes in searching it; she had shoved the fake to the bottom as well as she could.

* * *

She pulled the outer door shut behind her, checked that it was locked and shot down the stairs. None too soon. The dark figures were already in the courtyard. She dodged back and there was another stairway behind her — the one leading to the one apartment open to public view.

Without making any kind of plan, she hurried up the stairs and pushed a few coins to a pleasant looking girl sitting at a desk in the living room. These windows faced in a different direction entirely, back over the paved area. Once inside the cubes, it was difficult to gain any kind of sense of direction. Think. She had only seen the two men in the courtyard, not Danny. She looked round desperately but there was no view of the café. Was Danny still there? Or had they made him come with them? Of course they must have done. Where were they? She was looking down at an empty entrance-way, but was it the right one or were they inside Danny's flat by now? If so, she would have to risk leaving and hope for the best.

'You have finished? Already?' The girl seemed surprised.

'Very nice. Thank you very much.' She knew she was acting oddly which was unfortunate because the girl was sure to remember her if questioned, but it couldn't be helped. She dodged out and ran — back the way she and Danny had come and so moving away from the cafés around the harbour. But there was no way she was crossing over that vast paved space. She would be a sitting duck. She veered left along a main road, passing the glass roof of the Metro. Tempting, but if she had to wait on the platform, there would be nowhere to run if they caught up with her.

She glanced over her shoulder. How long would it take them to look through her abandoned bag and find the fake? Minutes, if that. And what then? Would they be fooled or would they realise there was another painting and that she had it? And whether they realised or not, Danny certainly would. She shivered.

How would he react to what she had done? Supposing he assumed she had taken the painting for herself? She gasped. Yes, of course, that would be exactly what he would think. Because it was the kind of thing *he* would do. She had to get rid of it somehow. She had to hand it over to the authorities as soon as she could. Only then would she be safe.

Stupid — why was she running? She was making herself conspicuous straightaway. Had she learned nothing during the past hours? She slowed to a walk. Be natural, she told herself.

That was the only way to merge with the crowds, if only there had been any. There was hardly anyone about at all. She thought longingly of the thronged alleyways of Delft; this road was in keeping with the whole space, wide and open. She had to get off it and seek some cover from buildings if there weren't any people.

How well had the men seen her features on the mobile phone photo? It wouldn't have been that clear with any luck. If only she'd thought to get a different top out of her bag. But even if she had thought of it, there had hardly been time for a change of clothes, however simple. Her thoughts were tumbling over themselves in panic.

At last, a turning — off to the left. And tallish buildings, white walls and small windows. Offices or something. This would do. She must find some concealed corner somewhere and she would study the map to see where the street was leading her.

Her heart was slowing a little now, thank goodness. And there were a few more people about. Tourists by the look of them. Not that there ever seemed to be many tourists about in Rotterdam but they must be going somewhere — so she followed the general direction.

Of course, this was the open-air section of the boat museum — the

Binnenvaart. Only this morning she had considered taking a look, since it was free. While she had waited for Danny. But she had come across the apartment on Coolsingel instead.

Danny. The memory was like a stabbing pain. What had he been trying to do? He had known, hadn't he, that the men would follow her? That had always been his intention. Even now he might be hurrying back happily to the cubehouse flat, with the coast clear, expecting to retrieve the padded bag from the table or the waste bin. Hadn't he cared what might happen to her when her pursuers caught up with her?

For the last time, she hardened her heart against him. Any last iota of guilt or feeling for him was gone. She doubted whether he had ever really loved her. He had kept on with the relationship while she could be useful to him. She had been nothing more than an innocent-looking courier.

Although maybe he had been keen for her opinions because of her second-hand knowledge of paintings from her ex-boyfriend, little enough though it was.

But what now? There was no time for self-pitying maundering. Even when she was out of all this, she didn't intend wasting her life on regrets. Her feet echoed on a gently bouncing wooden walkway over a canal.

Everything seemed so normal in the sunshine. Ahead and to the right, a small lighthouse marked the boat museum itself. Along a canal to the left were moored the extensive collection of historic boats. There must be plenty of places to hide here. She could see another main road from here too, leading to the graceful white towering structure of the Erasmus Bridge, nicknamed the Swan. Steven had told her that, she remembered with a pang. He had been chatting idly in the car on the way to Delft. Or maybe he had been trying to take her mind off what was to come. Thinking of her.

Where was he now? She should have

trusted him and stayed with him. She had left Steven for Danny, so intent on giving Danny every chance. She laughed bitterly. She had wanted to understand Danny and his motives. And now she knew too much about Danny and wished she didn't.

No, she must concentrate. Hiding here would be okay for now — but what next? She needed a quiet spot to sit and study the map and find the police station. She went up the gangplank of one of the nearer vessels, a turf barge apparently, and sat down to rest on the deck, her back propped against the warm planks of the low cabin. Her legs and back ached; she could have sat and dozed here forever. That would have to wait. She hoped the map would show the police station.

In fact, it showed too many. Would all these be manned? Perhaps some were just police phone boxes or something? This one by the town hall seemed the most likely to be the main headquarters, but it was way back — near the dim café where she and Danny had looked at the fake painting together. It would be.

Otherwise, there was one not too far away on the Witte de Withstraat. If she got onto that Erasmus Bridge road and walked back, the street in question would be off to her left. She would try that first and see. Could she get onto that road from here in the canal-side museum or would she have to back-track across the walkways? She stood up in order to see better, without thinking, and froze with horror.

* * *

They were there. Two black figures, one in a raincoat and one in a suit. They seemed to be looking straight at her. Keep calm. There were plenty of people about. How could they possibly recognise her, particularly if she gave no sign of there being anything wrong? They'd only seen a tiny mobile phone picture. She was merely an ordinary tourist studying a map. If she didn't do anything silly, they wouldn't know who she was.

Slowly, she folded the map and did what several other tourists were doing, stooping and stepping downwards through the low doorway leading to the interior of the barge. Now she was joining in a mini-lecture given by a charming Filipino guide. He was telling them where the family slept, what implements they had used, the purpose and function of turf barges — at any other time, Emma would have been fascinated. But now she was unable to concentrate. This was all very well — an excellent place to hide — but how long could she stay here?

In this enclosed space, the tour could only take ten minutes at most, she guessed, and then she would have to come out. Hoping the men had given up and moved on. She had followed her instincts but had she walked straight into a trap? She must get out of here and once out, wouldn't make that mistake again. Keep moving, that was the best way.

The tour was over. She joined the others in thanking the guide profusely; he seemed pleased although he obviously didn't speak any English and as he turned to a family group next to her, she tried to hang back and merge with them as they left. Where were the men? If they were between her and the road she wanted, that nearest police station would be too risky. If she phoned 999 — no, it was 112 here — how quickly would anyone respond? She glanced up and down the walkway. Which way should she go? Where would the wooden planks take her? Back the way she had come? At least she knew where that came out. She looked over to the right and saw Danny. He saw her in the same moment.

'Hey, wait!' He broke into a run. Even at this distance, she could almost feel his rage. And something else. It was a fury inspired by fear. She ran down the walkways, looking wildly from side to side. Masts, funnels, and a number of gangplanks leading into the welcoming sanctuary of living quarters. But no help there. She would be going straight into another trap. If she wasn't doing just that already. She groaned. Ahead of her, the walkway ended at open water. There was a sign that must mean you could catch a taxi here. In the distance small yellow water taxis were crossing the river.

She stopped at the edge. Behind her, Danny's steps paused, too. Like her, he could see there was nowhere to go. She turned and he was smiling. But not a pleasant smile. He was edging forwards towards her, arms outstretched as if gentling a frightened animal. He called out.

'It's okay. I only want that package you've got.'

'I know what's in it, Danny. You didn't tell me the truth.'

'Safer for you. I didn't want you putting yourself at risk.'

'That's a lie. You wanted those men

to come after me.' Among the boats at the other end of the walkway, a dark movement caught her eye. 'They're here now.'

'So we haven't much time, have we? Give it to me now and I'll lead them off. They're not interested in you.'

Do it, Emma thought. Take the easy option and be rid of it. Hand it over. But she was too angry with him to give in that easily. Too determined that he was not going to get away with this.

'I'm going to take it to the police,' she said defiantly.

'No! No need for that. It's a great idea, but I'll take it.'

'You've lied to me all along, haven't you?' She took a few steps back. How many more steps could she take? She was almost at the edge of the platform now. 'And it was never a gift from a grateful client. You stole it.'

'So what if I did? The old bat didn't know what it was. It was wasted on her.'

Why didn't he rush her? She had nowhere to go. Emma tensed, waiting for the swift sure movement where he would leap forwards and grab her and finish it. But, of course, she was too near the water. He couldn't risk damaging the painting. The painting had got her into this and caused all these problems, but now it was her only means of protection.

She glanced round. One of the yellow taxis was approaching at last. If she could only get it to stop here. If it worked like an ordinary land taxi . . . She waved. Keep him talking although it seemed a forlorn hope. Even if Danny didn't realise what she was doing, there wouldn't be enough time for her to get on board without him leaping on after her. But she couldn't think of anything else. For now, she must pretend to be going along with him.

'I don't know. Perhaps if you promised to give the money to the rightful owner. Those two are going to pay you, aren't they? They won't just take it. Or are they? How far can we trust them — because they won't feel like trusting you any more.' She took the backpack from her shoulders and pretended to be unzipping it. 'You had better be very sure, Danny. They're almost here.' Hardly surprising that she sounded so convincing. It was true. Thinking about the danger from Danny, she had not realised how close the others had come.

* * *

Danny risked a look round. And everything happened at once. She turned to summon the taxi again, knowing that the sound of the engine had been getting nearer and nearer. Now, it was sitting at the foot of the wooden jetty, bobbing gently up and down in the cool, clear waters.

And, no, it couldn't be. A face she had been longing to see — Steven.

'Jump, Emma,' he shouted. 'It isn't far.' She felt a burst of joy. He was here. Everything would be all right. Together, they could do this. Danny lunged as she jumped, still clutching the backpack. And Steven caught her. His arms were around her all too briefly. 'Right. Hang on.' He grabbed the controls and turned in a sharp circle that took her breath away. Spray drenched her face. She laughed.

'Have you ever driven one of these before?'

'Not often.'

They set off across the river at an angle. Too fast for her to ask questions. Where were they going? What about Danny? She looked back. A police boat passed them, going towards the landing stage and then another. Figures in uniform were converging on the three men.

'You'll have to make a statement, I'm afraid,' Steven said. 'And so will I.' The taxi had paused, circling, as they watched. Steven grinned. 'But not just yet. I've a taxi to return first. I bought the driver a meal at the hotel where I got on. In exchange for borrowing the boat for ten minutes.'

'A meal? It doesn't seem very much. Surely he would be putting his job on the line?'

'You'll see.' Steven grinned again.

'I'm sorry I ran,' Emma began by way of an apology. 'I didn't know who to trust.'

'I didn't do much to inspire your trust. My fault. This could have ended so badly. I should have taken better care of you. Since that was what I set out to do.'

'Hey, I can take care of myself!'

'I'm sure you can. But if I have my way, you won't need to.' More words were lost as he revved up the engine and they set off again.

'Where are we going?'

'After all this, you deserve the best. I'm going to see that you get it. I booked a table — one of the best eating places in town. Next stop, Hotel New Amsterdam.'

8

Emma clung on to her seat, hardly able to take everything in. Steven drove with a speed and skill that made thinking difficult. And one minute she had been pursued, certain that she was in danger, and now Steven was calmly telling her they were going out to eat? But now that he mentioned it, she had to admit that she was hungry. It was a long time since she had last eaten. Everything had been happening too quickly for Emma to think about food. But with the danger past, she realised that there was a gaping hole in her stomach.

She looked up at the imposing Victorian building ahead of them, with its red brick and ornamental stonework. This must be Hotel New Amsterdam. It would have dominated the river if it had not in its turn been overshadowed by the soaring shape of the Swan Bridge.

'Is it on an island?' she asked.

'No — although from the river it appears to be and many customers arrive by water. It used to be the offices of a shipping company. Well placed for that purpose. And today, it's very well placed for ours.'

Emma felt as if she were living in a dream. Emma in Wonderland. From nightmare to happiness in seconds. They recommended pinching yourself, didn't they, in these situations? But there wasn't time for that either. Steven was mooring the taxi and helping her out.

They entered the sumptuous restaurant, already filled with diners and with a word to the head waiter, Steven escorted her to a large, well-lit table near the windows.

There was someone sitting there already, a man in jeans and a sweater who grinned broadly as they approached, saying something in Dutch as he stood up. By the way he was gesturing at the table, Emma surmised that he was thanking Steven and agreeing that he had enjoyed himself. Yes, she could understand why a meal here might easily compensate for Steven's hire of the boat.

'This is Hans,' Steven said. 'Who has just earned my everlasting gratitude for his help.'

'You are okay? Now I meet you, I can understand this gentleman's urgency. But all went well?'

Emma wondered how much Steven had told him.

'Your taxi is over there.' Steven was saying. 'Safely returned, as agreed. And, here, these are to cover the return fare.' He handed the man a wad of money

'The meal would have been enough. I have always promised myself that one day, I would eat here. Thank you. All that was missing was a companion as beautiful as yours.' He gave a little bow of the head as he pocketed the notes. 'Enjoy your evening.'

'I'm sure we will.' Emma smiled. 'Thank you for everything.'

Almost without her noticing, during

their brief conversation the table had been quietly cleared and reset.

'Wow,' Emma said, 'this place is amazing.'

'Considered to be the most remarkable place to eat in Rotterdam. And the only place I could consider bringing such a remarkable girl. Is this table all right for you? There are some with a better view.'

'It's fine.' She laughed. 'Besides, the place is full. Or hadn't you noticed?' A mixed and cosmopolitan crowd of people and in spite of the splendour of the surroundings, she wasn't the only one in jeans and a simple top. Particularly at two or three tables in the far corner where she could see lighting equipment and wires. The diners there seemed to have surrounded themselves with laptops and cases and were very casually dressed. Obviously for them, this was a working meal. She assumed they must be a television crew. No one else seemed to be taking any notice of them; perhaps somewhere like this, it happened all the time.

'So it is. There were still a few tables left when I first came over and booked.'

He seemed very casual about his achievement but river views wouldn't be easy to obtain.

'I think you've worked miracles.' She smiled ruefully. 'Although I don't feel I'm dressed for this. Some of those women look absolutely amazing.'

'The Dutch pride themselves on being democratic. No one will mind what you wear. And, to me, you look pretty amazing yourself. I've thought so all day, from the first moment I saw you. I almost forgot what I was supposed to be doing when I came into that flat.'

'Did you know I would be there?' But thinking back to how they had first met reminded her that their adventure was not quite complete. 'And Steven — shouldn't you be making some kind of report to your superiors? And what about you-know-what?' She lowered her voice, resisting the temptation to pat her backpack.

He smiled with such warmth in his eyes that she was feeling weak all over again.

'You come first for me now — and always will. Statements and paperwork can wait. And you-know-what has waited in somebody's attic for hundreds of years, so another hour or two won't make much difference.' He shook his head. 'And, no, I didn't know you would be in Danny's flat. It was the first surprise of the day. A surprise that turned a routine police job into a wonderful experience.' He smiled, his eyes dancing. 'I knew when I first saw you, that one day — however far in the future that might have been — I would bring you here.'

'You seemed very certain that you would rescue me. Supposing it had gone wrong? And how did you know where I would be?'

'I knew Danny's friends were based on a boat moored a little way down the river. I hired the water taxi to keep a watch on it. If they found you, I knew they would take you there. I couldn't even contemplate not succeeding. I had to. In such a short time, you've become very special to me, Emma.'

Emma smiled.

'Even though I did my best to lose you at times?'

Steven shook his head.

'I admired your cleverness in getting rid of me even while I was very afraid for you. Shall we order? I think our waiter is hovering discreetly.'

Emma leaned back in her chair with a little sigh of contentment. She knew exactly what Steven meant. She too could feel the electric spark that flickered between them. A spark which might not need much encouragement to become something very important. She had never felt like this before. She was certain that she was on the brink of falling in love, if she hadn't already. Could it really happen this quickly? Yes, it could. How could she have ever deceived herself into thinking that she cared for Danny?

There was just one thing that was worrying her a little.

'Steven, when I left you in Delft . . . '

'Yes. I did wonder about that. At the time.'

'It was because you were talking to one of those men. The ones in the black we were trying to get away from.'

'Oh — no problem. My disguise meant I could get close up and have a good look at them and I realised I recognised one of them. One of my police contacts from several years ago. I thought I might be able to have a bit of a chat — and find out who he was working for now.'

'And did it work? Did he tell you?'

Steven shook his head.

'No. Said he was working as a private detective. And then I'd got myself into the situation of having to invent a reason for being there myself. In fact, we got ourselves into quite a complex conversation where he was offering to put in a word for me with his mythical agency. So I had to pretend that would be good and we parted on excellent terms, but without a word of truth said between us. And when I looked for you, there was no sign.'

'I saw you together and I didn't know what to think. I just ran.'

'I should have thought of how it would look to you. But I just seized the opportunity without thinking.'

'Never mind,' Emma said. 'It's all worked out for the best.' In fact, her experiences with Danny had proved once and for all that he couldn't be trusted. If she hadn't set off on her own, she might not have gained the indisputable proof of what Danny was. She would always have wondered whether she'd done the right thing.

The waiter brought wine and small snacks and Emma was floating in a warm bubble, she and Steven together. Their hands touched across the table. He was looking into her eyes.

'What did Danny really mean to you?' he asked.

A warm shiver of happiness crossed her spine. Again, it was as if Steven had been sharing her thoughts.

'Not very much. As I told you, I'd begun to realise that. When he betrayed me I realised he only wanted to make use of me. I knew I was making the right decision.'

'I needed to be sure — because you are so important to me.' He grinned. 'I've only known you for a matter of hours and here I am putting my heart on my sleeve as my grandmother would have said. I don't usually do that, either. I'm known for being very deliberate. But I have to tell you how I feel.'

'I feel the same way,' Emma said softly. Perhaps the heady excitement of the last hours was influencing her. That was what they always said about war romances, didn't they? How the danger and excitement exaggerated feelings and brought people together with a sense of urgency. And yet she was certain her instincts were telling her the truth.

She had never felt this way about Danny, or anyone else. It wasn't only the excitement of being with this man. She sensed that you could feel safe with Steven. And yet it would never be a dull kind of safe.

The food was wonderful and yet almost wasted on Emma that evening. She was hardly noticing what she ate, beyond being vaguely aware that everything was delicious. All her attention was on Steven. Drinking in everything about him, the way he laughed, the way the expressions crossed his strong and angular face. She never wanted this evening to end.

Somewhere outside their bubble, the waiter coughed. Steven released her hand as they turned to look up at him.

'Excuse me, sir, madam — but if you have finished your meal, Mr van Lek would like to meet you.' Emma frowned, puzzled. She didn't recognise the name at first. The waiter was holding a circular silver tray towards them with two small cards, one each,

Emma supposed. She took one and saw a name and also a photograph. A face that seemed familiar and seeing the name in print made it easier to understand what the waiter had said.

'Oh! Yes, Mr van Lek, the philanthropist.' He had been all over the newspapers at the station and the man in the tourist information office had mentioned him, too. Was it only that morning? It seemed like days ago.

The waiter nodded, smiling.

'A good man. He is in the Premier Suite. If you wish, I can — '

'I know who he is, thank you.' Steven was frowning uncharacteristically.

'I wonder why he should want to see us?' Emma murmured.

'I don't know. We don't have to go . . . '

There was a flicker of alarm in the waiter's eyes.

'Mr van Lek was most insistent.'

'Of course we'll come,' Emma said. 'We don't want anyone to get into trouble. That's not fair.'

Steven paused briefly and then nodded.

'You're right. And I think I know what this is about.' He turned to the waiter who was beginning to fidget. 'I'll come and see him. The young lady will wait here.'

'I'm sorry, sir, but the gentleman was clear. The young lady is invited also.'

Emma laughed.

'That isn't a problem. I'm coming, too.'

Steven hesitated, and looked rather nervous as he spoke.

'I didn't want you to get involved with this. Not yet. Although obviously you will eventually. It's a family thing.'

'Really?' Her eyes widened in surprise.

Steven was already standing, to the waiter's obvious relief and Emma rose, too.

'This man is my father,' he said in a low voice.

Emma stared at him.

'But everyone knows him. Even I've

heard of him and I've only just got here. And I thought you were English.' They began to follow the waiter through the packed tables and out into the foyer.

'He has a huge profile in the Netherlands, yes. But I haven't seen him for years. He left us, in England, when I was a child. I use my mother's name. Not his.'

'So this meeting will be difficult for you. Steven, I don't want to intrude.'

Steven gave a short laugh. 'It seems to be what he wants. And for me, no way will you being there be an intrusion. I just don't want you to be subjected to any unpleasantness.'

'Anything that affects you affects me, Steven. That's the way I want it.' The waiter ushered them into the lift. There was little opportunity for saying anything personal now. Emma felt for Steven's hand and he smiled at her. Yes, the lift was sliding silently up to the topmost floor — but what else would you expect? As the doors opened, the waiter stood back and a man in a smart, dark suit was there to welcome them. All these men in dark suits, Emma thought, she was getting neurotic about them. Perhaps it was a Dutch thing. No time to worry about that.

The man's smile was pleasant as he ushered them into an opulent suite of rooms, filled with light. At any other time, Emma would have been drinking in the luxurious hangings and furnishings, but now her attention was focussed on the room's only occupant.

A man who was seated to face them as they entered, and behind him were large windows opening onto a balcony. With this arrangement, he could clearly see their faces while his own was hidden in shadow, but Emma would have recognised the features anywhere. Of course, he seemed familiar from the photos, but meeting him face to face, she was now struck by his resemblance to Steven. The small beard made the most obvious difference and the hair was greying, but the strength of the jaw was the same.

He rose easily and came forward, his hand outstretched.

'At last. You are most welcome. Both of you. Thank you for complying with my summons.' The words and tone gave the impression that he was sharing a joke at his own expense. Emma usually enjoyed that quality in people and should have warmed to him. But the ultra-strong handshake and something hidden in the blue eyes made her uneasy.

'A pleasure to meet you, Steven, after so long,' he was saying. 'And in the company of such a delightful young lady.'

'The length of time has been nothing to do with me,' Steven said calmly. 'Not at first. It was your choice. And later, there seemed no need to seek a meeting.'

The man smiled sadly.

'No purpose in dwelling on the past. Better to move forward.'

'Indeed. What do you want?'

Emma almost gasped at Steven's sudden hostility, but Mr van Lek seemed unperturbed. She would have expected anger — or at least disappointment. That reaction more than anything else, made her trust Steven's assessment of the situation.

It was as if the smile was fixed to van Lek's face.

'Why would I want something? I seek only to help you, in whatever way I can. And the family connection, although fascinating, is not why I wanted to meet you.' Suddenly he turned to face Emma and she gave a small start at becoming the focus of attention. 'I believe we have a mutual acquaintance, Emma.'

9

How did he know her name? And how did he know they would be dining in the hotel anyway? And why had Steven made this choice? Wouldn't it have been better to hand the painting over straightaway? Her hand tightened on her backpack. Suddenly she was no longer sure of anything again and the resulting wave of pain almost made her cry out.

'Oh, Emma, my dear,' Mr van Lek said. 'What an expressive face you have.'

Mutual acquaintance. Hang on. There was only one other person in Rotterdam she knew.

'You must mean Danny? How do you know him?'

'Indeed I do mean your friend Danny. And to answer your second question — sometimes he can be of use to me. He has certainly proved himself useful in the past. And on this occasion he had promised me that he would be even more so. But as you and I know, Danny is not all that he seems. He doesn't always say what he means, which makes life difficult for those who thought they could trust him. But you are obviously a young lady of great good sense. You have seen through him. And I admire the courage and initiative you have demonstrated since your arrival in Rotterdam.'

'You haven't changed, have you?' Steven said bitterly. 'Where is this going?'

Even before he answered, Emma knew — with a sudden flash of insight that came too late. Mr van Lek's liking for surrounding himself with men in dark suits had become only too clear. That was why the man by the lift had seemed familiar.

But had Steven really not known that the man behind the day's pursuit had been his father? She turned to look at him, hating to be even thinking the question, but the fury in Steven's face surely proved his innocence. Perhaps, like herself so many times that day, he had not wanted to recognise the unwelcome truth.

Mr van Lek gave a little bow of the head in acknowledgement. 'It is high time we got together and sorted everything out to our mutual advantage. Because, I believe, in spite of the day's unfortunate misunderstandings, we all have the same aims.'

'I could never have the same aims as you,' Steven growled.

No, thank goodness. But even as Emma felt the sweet glow of relief, she realised the danger they were in. Unwittingly, they had entered the very trap they had tried so hard to avoid. Van Lek wanted the painting. Of course, he was the mystery customer Danny had been trying to do business with. Or to defraud — which was even more dangerous. She had been so stupid in not seeing it before. Once again, she had ignored what had been under her nose because she didn't want to believe it. She could have kicked herself.

There was no time for wishing she had worked things out better and done something else. She didn't like this, any of it. But she had to concentrate on what they were going to do next. And how they could get themselves out of this. Perhaps all was not lost. Meeting van Lek's politely worded request with angry defiance was tempting but Emma knew instinctively that it wouldn't help. She took a deep breath.

'And those aims are?' she asked smoothly.

'Emma, don't,' Steven begged. There was anguish in his voice.

She desperately wanted him to understand what she was trying to do. She raised her eyebrows at him, smiling confidently.

'I don't see why not.' She hated having to try this. Supposing Steven believed her? She felt anguish at even attempting it. But it was the only way she could think of, to gain the time they needed.

His father nodded approvingly.

'A young lady of sense. You may learn from her, Steven. Yes, my dear, you have something I want.'

'And that is?' She needed time to think, to try to work something out. She just hoped that Steven would get it. 'I don't know what you can possibly mean.' A pity she hadn't thought to pass the painting to Steven. With all the attention on her, he might have managed some evasive action. It would have been small enough to be carried safely beneath his jacket. Just. You could almost think, the way he was holding his jacket bundled awkwardly over his arm, that he had the painting already.

'Come now. We both know you have the undiscovered Vermeer. You, I presume, are selling. I am willing to buy. I will give you a good price, I can assure you. And no questions asked.'

'No questions asked?' Emma said carefully. 'But it isn't mine to sell.' She frowned for a moment. 'I suppose it belongs to Danny.' He had more or less admitted, hadn't he, that he had been lying about that?

No doubt it would be his word against hers and the old lady might have no clear idea of what had gone on. False pretences and fraud might well come into it somewhere if the police were to take a long hard look at that.

Mr van Lek laughed. 'Danny? We both know that he must have gained it by dubious means — however he may have tried to justify himself. He will be no trouble. But I can add a certain amount to keep him quiet if you like. A substantial amount.' He smiled and Emma wondered how she could ever have considered him likeable. 'See how generous I can be when I know what I want.' He lowered his voice and his tone became menacing. 'And I always get what I want, Emma. Make no mistake about that.' His eyes flickered sideways and behind her. She could sense the man in the suit moving forwards a little.

Oh, please, Steven, she thought. *Catch on to what I'm trying to do*.

Steven's face was grim, giving nothing away. She had a horrible feeling that he was being taken in by her act. If so, he already believed he could no longer trust her. Would he ever trust her again?

Emma let her fingers drop behind her back, fluttering in what she hoped was a frantic gesture of denial and that Steven would pick up on it.

'And what will you do with the painting?' she said to van Lek.

At first, Steven didn't move and then, yes, he had realised. He was edging away, making his way towards the window, where the evening sun was flooding in from the balcony.

Emma kept her face straight with an effort although she felt like grinning with relief. She didn't think anyone else had spotted the gradual movement. Steven was still near enough to be a part of the conversation if necessary — or to offer a protective barrier between her and his father. He couldn't have placed himself more advantageously if she had been able to discuss it with him directly. Because a plan was forming at last. She could see what they could do, working together. And it might just come off . . .

* * *

Mr van Lek didn't seem to have noticed anything. But, of course, he hardly knew Steven now. She was more in tune with his son than he was. The older man laughed.

'You ask what I shall do with the painting? I shall enjoy it, of course. What else might one do with an object of such quality? The knowledge that it belongs to me alone will be very precious to me. And that only I in the whole world may appreciate it. That is what I am willing to pay for.'

'It's okay, Emma,' Steven said suddenly. 'It's going to be all right.'

Van Lek laughed again.

'Well done. How very civilised. I knew you would help us to see reason. You are my son, after all.'

Emma gave Steven a long, considering look, as if she were seeking advice or reassurance.

'How much are you offering?' she asked, hardly turning her head to van Lek.

'Well, my dear, I will not insult you by offering too little.' He was obviously enjoying himself now. 'The last Vermeer to go on sale, several years ago, brought sixteen million. But I feel now that the time has come for me to actually see what is on offer, don't you?'

Emma froze. What? How much had he said? She was hardly able to take in the amount. And she had been running round Rotterdam with something worth that much in her bag? She pulled herself together abruptly. Time enough to worry about that if and when they got out of this.

Steven twitched his jacket awkwardly, as if concealing something beneath it.

He took a couple more steps sideways. Emma felt a warm wave of love and relief. Yes, he understood. They had a chance. She reached for her backpack, holding it firmly in both hands. They were all watching her; even the bodyguard behind her was edging forwards. She tensed and shouted abruptly.

'Now, Steven! Throw it out of the window. To Danny.' And Steven was leaping out onto the balcony, holding his jacket in front of him as if something was being held and protected within the fabric. She didn't wait to see what he did next. In those few seconds, van Lek turned, shouting, his face white with shock and anger. The bodyguard threw himself towards Steven and another guard rushed in from the corridor.

It was enough. They had all forgotten her. But she knew she had only moments before they realised how they had been tricked. Besides, even if they still believed the painting was inside the jacket, they would run to the stairs to retrieve it at ground level.

Quickly she stepped backwards, out into the corridor. Yes, the lift was there, still waiting. She rushed in and the doors closed behind her. She had gained a last brief picture of the scene within the room but already, one man was turning, and with something in his hand — a gun? She gasped in horror as they began to move downwards. So slowly that she could have screamed. Two floors passed. Three. The lift stopped, but they were nowhere near ground level. The doors were opening and it was too soon. Oh, no. An elderly couple stepped in, smiling. How long would it take desperate men to lunge down the stairs? Without thinking, Emma shot out of the lift, leaving surprised faces behind her.

'Sorry,' she called. But already the lift and its passengers were sweeping downwards without her. The second lift was coming upwards towards her; for a moment her fingers hovered over the button. No, too easy for the men to see where the lifts were and be waiting for her. She had been lucky to get away with it once.

There were the stairs. She peered cautiously through the glass panel in the fire door, leading to the stairwell. No, already she could hear pounding footsteps on the staircase above her; she dodged back just in time. How many men were there? Two passed as she watched through the glass panel and yet here was a third coming. She didn't think van Lek would be taking part in the pursuit himself. Not when he employed so many people to leap to his bidding. Unless? She risked another glimpse through the door and now saw Steven flashing past. Obviously he was making a brave effort to protect her. She pressed a hand over her mouth because the temptation to call out to him was so strong. But if she did, the others would hear her — and also hear him stopping to answer her and that would ruin everything. At least when she reached the ground floor, Steven would be there, too. The thought warmed her because she knew what she was going to do.

But for now she needed a way down and both the lifts and these stairs were too risky. She glanced up and down the corridor and, yes, that was what she needed. A door at the end with a fire exit sign on it. She had assumed that a hotel of his calibre would have a staff staircase. And if it turned out to be alarmed, that would be more than welcome. She needed to attract the attention of the general public, the more people the better. But, no, it wasn't, because she pushed the door and it opened without setting anything off.

Now she must concentrate on getting herself all the way down, as fast as possible. She thought she could hear distant shouts. From the foyer maybe? She passed a surprised chambermaid, her arms filled with towels and saw the look of astonishment on her upturned face as Emma flashed past. That was close, she had only narrowly avoided bumping into the girl. And then she was down, with only another doorway in front of her. She opened the door carefully, just an inch, panting as she peered through the narrow gap. There was no one in the foyer, but, yes, through the glass entrance doors she could see there were dark figures outside, scanning the waterfront and staring upwards. They were looking for her, maybe even looking for Danny. She had almost forgotten that part of her trick and that she had pretended to call out to him, but obviously her pursuers hadn't. While they were occupied out there, she was safe.

* * *

She set off across the large marble-floored vastness of the space, trying to walk briskly but naturally. Trying to remember which way they had come as they followed the waiter and very aware now that she was hardly dressed to blend in. She could see Steven by the doors, making sure the two henchmen didn't come in again. She grinned at him.

And then everything happened at once. Behind her, the chambermaid she had passed came hurrying out, gesturing to the manager who was now approaching her purposefully. Of course, the girl would think Emma must be a thief. She had raised the alarm. And at the same time, one of the men dodging around outside turned and saw her. He shouted to the other one. As they erupted back through the doors, Steven deliberately cannoned into them, knocking them both off balance as he fell with them.

She heard him shout, 'Keep going, Emma.' And the restaurant lay ahead.

She knew what she wanted to see. Would they still be there? They had to be. And yes, the lights were switched on and the camera crew were in full swing, interviewing a blonde girl in a white dress. No time to worry too much about her. Although no doubt the resulting publicity wouldn't do her career any harm. Emma's limbs seemed to be moving incredibly slowly, as if she was wading though mud.

At last. She had made it. Surprised faces were turning to stare at her. Emma struggled to open her backpack, and running forward, thrust the painting in front of the camera.

'I have discovered an unknown painting by Vermeer,' she said loudly and triumphantly. 'And, on behalf of Mr van Lek, it is to be donated to the nation.'

10

Almost a year had passed and it was another hot summer when Emma and Steven once again travelled over to Rotterdam. This time they had a special visit to make. They could have accepted the official invitation of three weeks before, but their wedding and honeymoon had taken precedence. Conveniently so. There was no way either of them wanted to meet van Lek again. Now they stood, hand in hand, gazing silently at the painted face, securely in her rightful place on the wall of the gallery.

'You wouldn't know she caused so much trouble,' Steven said. 'She looks so calm.'

Emma smiled.

'She's concentrating — yet there's more to her. You wonder what she's thinking.' Emma looked around the vastness of the room in the gallery. *Woman Kneading Dough* was a popular attraction at the moment, with all the publicity, but for now they had her to themselves. 'I'm glad we avoided all the fuss.'

They had seen the coverage on TV — one of Emma's sisters had recorded it for them, so Emma knew that van Lek had made the best of his unexpected 'donation'. You wouldn't have thought he had ever had anything else in mind.

And, on Emma's insistence, the original owner, the elderly lady Danny had defrauded, had been traced, given a suitable payment and made a guest of honour. Her joy and delight more than made up for van Lek's pomposity.

'There was no need for us to be there anyway,' Emma said. 'We were only go-betweens.'

'Besides, it's good that *Woman Kneading Dough* is back where she belongs — but for me there was something far more important that came out of all that. Better than any painting, however valuable.' Steven squeezed her hand.

'Really?' Emma laughed, knowing that Steven realised she was teasing him. 'What would that be?'

'Meeting you. The love of my life.'

'Oh, yes,' Emma agreed. 'It was worth it. The danger, the fear — even if we had lost her, I would still have had you. She changed my life.' Emma glanced at the painting. No wonder the woman was smiling. Perhaps she had known from the first. And, now, she was the only witness as they kissed — and Emma forgot everything.

Other titles in the
Linford Romance Library:

THE BUTTERFLY DANCE

Rosemary A. Smith

It's 1902 and life, for Katherine Johnson, has been rather mundane, living with her Aunt Phoebe and Uncle Zachariah in their house on the coast. However, on her twentieth birthday, she meets Kane O'Brien on the beach and suddenly her thoughts are all of him. But will the circumstances of Kane's birth prevent her Aunt from accepting their love for one another? What is the mystery of the beautiful keepsake box? And where will the butterfly dance lead them?

LONG SHADOWS

Margaret Mounsdon

When Fiona Dalrymple's grandmother dies, Fiona is shocked to learn that Doreen wasn't actually her grandmother at all . . . Her grandfather's first wife, Ellie Marsden, is still alive and when Fiona meets her, Ellie has a further shock for Fiona: she also has a brother. What's more, Tim has disappeared and Fiona is charged with the task of finding him . . . so why does Rory, Tim's handsome boss, seems intent on being more of a hindrance than a help?

LEAVING HOME

Cara Cooper

Flora Canning's bags are packed. She's ready to begin a fresh life in New York, leaving her handsome friend Richard Cross devastated at her departure. But plans don't always work out, and a family tragedy forces Flora to stay a while longer. Then fabulously wealthy Nate Campbell enters her life with an offer most women couldn't refuse, and Flora has to learn who to trust and whether it is better to rule with your head or with your heart.

PERILOUS MASQUERADE

Stella Kent

Linda would do anything for her sister — she'd had her fair share of problems. But Julia's unusual request resulted in Linda having to work in Greece, posing as the mother of her nephew, Nickie. It was a perilous masquerade, but for the child's sake — and Julia's — she daren't let the mask slip. But when she found herself falling in love with Andrew Duncan, her boss, how she wished that she could reveal her true identity, and her feelings.

A BRIDE FOR LORD MOUNTJOY

Karen Abbott

Georgiana's unchaperoned childhood ends when her father discovers her returning from a midnight jaunt with her brother and his friends. Squire Hailsham sends Georgiana to the Highpark Academy for Young Ladies in Brighton. There she enters High Society, where she attends elegant balls and meets dashing heroes. At the onset of a family tragedy, the eligible Lord Mountjoy crosses her path — but is he all that he seems? Does Georgiana risk breaking her heart when she discovers the truth?